REAP

THE IRISH MOB CHRONICLES

KAYE BLUE

Reap

Copyright © 2017 Kaye Blue

www.kayebluewriter.com/newsletter

WRITER OF MEN WHO THRILL

WWW.KAYEBLUEWRITER.COM/NEWSLETTER

Join for all the latest news on
Kaye and her books!

Sign up for Kaye's Newsletter to get all the latest
news about her books!

WHEN LOVERS COLLIDE...

HER STUBBORNNESS CHALLENGES ME. HER CURVES TEMPT ME. SHE'S MINE—WHETHER SHE KNOWS IT OR NOT. AND WHEN DANGER CALLS, ALL BETS ARE OFF...

MY BROTHER THINKS I'm a hothead, and since he's in charge, I'm on the sidelines. Stuck babysitting a hotel that's beset by a million small problems when we have real business to handle.

Bad enough—but with her it gets so much worse.

Eden.

She's supposed to be my assistant general manager. Instead she's a pain in my ass. Challenging me at every turn like she has no idea who my family is. Stubbornness and pure aggravation wrapped in curves that I'm having a hard time resisting.

And I can't afford distractions. Those small problems have gotten a lot bigger. Someone's setting me up...and they're targeting Eden too.

Time to unleash the kind of holy hell that hotheads like me are best at.

ONE

EDEN

"No."

I kept my gaze on Michael Murphy after I had uttered the word, though it took everything inside of me not to look away.

If his expression was anything to go by, Michael was angry, something that wasn't at all uncommon for him.

He was also questioning my sanity.

A question we shared.

At least in my professional life, I thought of myself as prudent, reasonable, but I seemed to lose sight of all those qualities in Michael's presence. Something about him, the arrogant tilt of his head, the way he demanded obedience, absolute respect, like it was something he was owed, pissed me off, made me cast prudence aside and antagonize him.

It was risky, defying Michael like that. Foolish, too, considering he was technically my employer.

And a mobster.

"What did you say?" he asked.

I almost blinked, his bland, disinterested tone nearly throwing me off my stride. I instantly recognized it for the warning sign it was, the clue that Michael was close to his breaking point.

Funny that.

Michael wasn't above yelling, at least at me, something I had no problem returning in kind. But when that tone got thrown into the mix, the casual, smooth whisper that was more appropriate for seduction than a business meeting, I knew I was on dangerous ground.

It was definitely time for me to back away, but stubbornness—and the thrill of pushing Michael just a bit farther—wouldn't let me.

I kept my eyes centered on his, ignored the little thud my heart gave—and the reason my heart gave it—and spoke.

"I said no."

The withering glare he gave me should have sent me running away screaming, would have if he were someone else. But he was Michael, and I was unwilling to give even an inch, despite how common sense told me I should.

Because as withering as his expression was, there was also expectation in it, his firm belief that I would bend to his will. I hated that, and even more, refused to give in to it.

Childish? Yes.

Stupid? Yes.

Unavoidable? God, yes.

So instead of apologizing, walking that no back, or at least softening my position, I stayed exactly where I was, back ramrod straight, chubby legs crossed at the ankles, my uniform's skirt lying primly over my knees, my eyes lasered on his, the night-sky blue now stormy.

"Do you want to reconsider your answer?" he asked, even blander now, almost polite.

A shudder rocked through me, involuntary and uncontrollable.

Michael was not polite, *ever*, and when I considered the storm in his eyes and the blandness of his voice, I marveled that he was managing to hold his temper at all.

Still, as ill-conceived as this may be, I had a point to prove.

"No, I don't want to reconsider. I heard your request, thought about it, and made my decision. I'm not going to do it," I said.

I tried to keep my voice as bland as Michael's, though I doubted I could pull off the look. His dark hair was swept back, his hand-sewn shirt open at the neck, his overall appearance more that of a bored aristocrat than revealing what he actually was. Yeah, there was no way I, in my hotel-issued blazer and loafers could match his superior, disinterested tone. But that didn't mean I wouldn't make the effort.

Effort Michael noticed.

His eyes got stormier, and I could see the edges of his control beginning to fray.

"I believe we have a misunderstanding, Eden," he said, speaking slowly, sounding almost patient, not that I'd ever believe Michael Murphy could be patient.

"Which is?" I asked, portraying an ignorance that he didn't buy, one that probably only served to piss him off more.

That thought made me want to smile, made my heart beat a little harder. Awoke other places too, places that I had no business thinking about here in the presence of a man I was pretty sure I hated.

However, I ignored all those thoughts, focused on Michael.

"Which is," he said, drawing out the words, his eyes narrowing into little slits as he spoke, "you think you have a choice in the matter. This is my hotel. You work for me, Eden. So you'll do as I say."

His voice had taken on an edge now, one that again made me shiver, again for all the wrong reasons. I should have been furious, was furious, actually. But, as shameful as it was to admit, I was enjoying this, knew I would replay every look, every moment, every word back later.

I ignored that though, and focused on what was happening now. Michael was being ridiculous, and I refused to back down.

"Yes, I am your employee. But I was also given final say over personnel in this hotel. I'm not going to dismiss those security guards," I said.

I looked down, needing a break from the intensity of his gaze, the intensity of my reaction to it, and braced myself for Michael's response.

When he stayed silent, I glanced up at him, curious. About the fact that he hadn't responded yet, about the fact that we were having this conversation at all.

Michael had never seemed that interested in

personnel, typically leaving the hiring and firing, and most of the other operations of the hotel, to me and Gerald Collins, the hotel's general manager. That he was pressing this particular decision was of note, something I'd lost sight of while I'd been distracted with Michael's and my little game.

It was time to refocus on business.

"Maybe if you could explain—"

"Explain myself to you, Eden?" he said. That blandness was gone, and his voice was now a low hiss, one that made it impossible to miss how angry he was, not that I had.

I froze for a moment, his apparent scorn taking me aback and sapping some of the energy and excitement of this conversation. I should be used to this by now, had known it was coming, but every time Michael looked at me like that, used that tone that confirmed he thought very little of me, it got to me.

I knew better, had known where this was headed, but I'd pushed, and again was paying for it. I liked to think of these little standoffs as games, and often, they were just that. But other times... Michael's words, his tone, shouldn't have the power to hurt me, should have just rolled off. At this moment though, they stung. I ignored that bite of hurt, tried to keep my mind focused on the matters at hand.

"Very well, Michael," I said, calling on my years of customer service experience to keep all emotion out of my voice. "There's no need to explain if you don't want to, but I'm not comfortable dismissing such long-standing employees without at least some idea of what they've done wrong."

And everything else aside, that was true. Michael wanted to take away those guards' livelihoods, something I wouldn't let happen, not without a good reason.

One look at Michael, and I could see that both my rock-solid reasoning and my attempt to placate him had fallen flat.

"Get out," he said.

I stood and headed toward the office door, and met Sean Murphy, one of Michael's brothers and one of my four bosses, at the door.

I looked at him, saw the smile in his green eyes. "So somebody's being an ass today, I take it?" he asked.

I smiled, but didn't speak, knowing confirmation wasn't necessary, which drew a laugh from Sean. "That face says it all, Eden," he said.

"Morning, Sean," I said by way of answer.

"Good morning, beautiful," he replied, adding a little wink.

"Still an outrageous flirt, I see," I said.

"Is it working?" he asked.

"Nope," I replied with a smile.

Sean put his hand on his heart, shook his head. "It's barely after breakfast, and I've already been shattered. Looks like I'm in for a long day."

"You'll survive," I said, smiling even brighter now, something that was easy to do with Sean, who couldn't have been more different than Michael in looks and temperament.

"You were leaving, weren't you, Eden?" Michael said.

My smile dropped, and it took all the self-control I had not to flip him off. From the twinkle in Sean's eye, I could see he noticed.

"I'll see you, Sean," I said tightly, and left.

As I got farther away from the office, my heart started to slow, the comedown from the adrenaline rush leaving me shaky.

For almost two years now, Michael Murphy never failed to have that effect on me.

One minute we'd be going toe to toe, the next, he'd drop some obnoxious comment or dismiss me out of hand. He made me so angry, as mad as anyone ever had, but no matter what, whenever I left his presence, I felt alive in a way I never did anywhere else.

Yet, I still had no idea why.

It wasn't looks.

Michael was unequivocally, undeniably, impossibly handsome, the most handsome of the Murphys to my eyes. He'd won the genetic lottery, standing at a towering six five, all of him pure muscle. His features were perfection, so perfect, in fact, that he sometimes looked surreal.

He was also rude, domineering, arrogant, and, quite frankly, an asshole.

I hated assholes.

And yet…

I didn't hate Michael.

Or didn't *only* hate him.

He was the single most infuriating person I'd ever met, had the ability to drive me into a rage with something as simple as a tilt of his head.

I also wanted him with an intensity that took my breath away, one that had led to far too many sleepless nights spent craving someone I could never have and shouldn't even want.

A desire that only grew stronger the more I tried to resist it.

I adjusted my blazer as I walked down the hall leading away from the executive office suite, anxious to do something with that excess energy that being around Michael always left me with.

I'd never freely confess it, but this *thing* with him was becoming a distraction, one made all the worse because it was so one-sided. In a perverse way, it might have given me a small sense of pride if I could say that Michael took unique pleasure in annoying me, but I didn't even have that to hold onto.

Sure, he was a jerk to me, but he was a jerk to everyone, even his brothers. There was nothing special in that. Worse, he was responsible for hurting one of the people I cared about most in the world. All that should have been enough, more than, to kill the silly and unreciprocated attraction to him, especially when I considered his family's reputation, the rumors about who they were and what they did. But the disconnect between my brain and my body when it came to Michael Murphy was strong, and so far, my body was winning, that attraction to him as potent as any I'd ever felt.

I adjusted my jacket once more and then plastered a smile on my face as I walked into the front lobby.

I had a job to do, and Michael fucking Murphy wouldn't stop me.

TWO

MICHAEL

"HAVE I ever told you how much I like Eden?" Sean asked, his shit-eating grin making me want to take a swing at him. I glared at him, but most of my ire was directed at her.

"Only every time you see her," I responded through gritted teeth, prepping myself for what I knew would come next. Sean singing Eden's praises like everyone else did, making me think of her when she wasn't around, like I didn't do that enough as it was.

"Yeah," Sean said, his entire face bright as he continued without pause, "she's fucking awesome, mostly because she takes no shit from you."

Don't take the bait, Michael.

I whispered that over and over in my head until the urge to respond was finally gone.

Sean, annoying shit that he was, knew exactly what buttons to push, but I was getting better at not falling for it. Impressive, especially since I was still wound up from going toe to toe with Eden.

I grimaced, and Sean laughed, leaving no doubt that he knew exactly what—who—I was thinking about.

The very idea of going toe to toe with Eden was fucking ridiculous. She was my hotel's assistant general manager, a curvy little slip of a woman who should have given me no trouble at all. A stern glare should have been enough to melt her, make her eager to do exactly as I said.

But it never had been.

Eden tossed off the stern glares I enforced my direct commands with like they were nothing.

Me, the Murphy brother most renowned for my temper, my unyielding nature. My absolute requirement for unquestioned obedience.

Yet almost every encounter with Eden ended as a stalemate. It was sickening.

And more of a turn-on than anything I'd experienced in years.

I snapped the pen I'd been holding in two, then quickly dropped it, watched as the dark ink stained the papers on my desk.

"Wow, she really got you good," Sean said.

"What the fuck do you want?" I asked, not bothering to look at Sean as I discarded the broken pen and stained papers, but knowing he was right and that he knew it too.

"I came to talk business. Perfect timing from the look of it," he responded.

"Let's go," I said.

Sean nodded, and we both stood and made our way out of the executive suites.

As we passed out of the office area, I saw Eden out of the corner of my eye. A bright, pleasant smile was plastered on her face as she spoke with one of the guests, the dazzling white of her teeth beautiful against her brown skin.

She never smiled at me, something that pissed me off, though not as much as the fact that I noticed.

I took some solace in the fact that Eden seemed to be doing her best not to look at me, knew that whether she looked at me or not, she noticed me.

I could see the slight change in her posture when I entered the lobby, saw the way she put visible effort into keeping her eyes from tracking me.

Wouldn't it be nice if Eden was keeping her gaze down too because she had realized the folly of continually opposing me?

There wasn't a fucking chance of that.

The more likely answer was that she was putting on a demure act, slipping into a role that she seemed to use with everyone but me.

It fit, too.

With others, Eden was reasonable, kind. She always had a warm smile, genuine concern for every guest and employee of the hotel. I couldn't count the number of birthdays she'd remembered, flowers she'd sent, times she'd gone out of her way just to make sure people knew they were valued.

I could have understood if that warmth didn't extend to the Murphys. It had taken the staff a while to get used to the new ownership, and Eden was no exception. But it wasn't that. Just last month, she'd sent my brother Patrick a flower arrangement to celebrate his wedding, and she'd sent Sean a birthday card.

What did I get?

I got ice-cold eyes, rigid posture, and a "no"

delivered by usually lush lips that were shaped into a thin, almost angry line.

It drove me insane, something I wouldn't dare admit, but something that was nonetheless true.

I wouldn't be defeated, though. Eden would see the error of her ways, eventually.

As we got farther away from the executive suite, my thoughts turned from Eden. It was a temporary break; she'd be back in them soon enough. But by the time we'd reached the bowels of the hotel, the place we went to speak freely, I'd managed to push aside thoughts of Eden long enough to focus.

I looked at Sean, who was serious now.

"Everything's good, right?" I asked.

"Yeah. I just want to make sure I stay in touch," he said.

Reasonable, given what had happened a couple of months ago. Patrick had been ambushed in the hotel, and though we had taken care of that problem, we were all still on alert, so it was good of Sean to stay in touch.

"No news here, except..." I trailed off, something that was uncharacteristic of me, something that didn't go unnoticed by my brother.

"Except what?" he asked.

"It's been a couple of months since that shit

with Patrick. Long enough to get rid of the security guards," I said.

"They didn't have anything to do with it, right?"

"No, but they were incompetent. That's more than enough cause to get rid of them," I said.

"So get rid of them," Sean said.

"I would, but Patrick gave Eden control over the employees," I replied, my anger rising.

I looked at Sean and saw the dawning realization on his face as he smiled.

"And she's not doing what you say?"

"Does she ever?" I spat, then quickly went quiet, not wanting my frustration to show through.

"Seems not. So why not force the issue?" he said.

I didn't bother to explain that forcing the issue with Eden would be a fool's errand and one that would probably drive me insane. She was the most stubborn person I had ever met, including myself.

Instead, I said, "I don't want to draw undue attention."

"Meaning?" he asked.

"Meaning she's going to ask why I'm insisting, and that's not a conversation I want to have," I said.

"That's probably smart. So just let it go," Sean said.

Even thinking about doing so put my teeth on edge. I shouldn't have to explain myself to Eden, and she should do as I say.

"Maybe," I said.

"So you're definitely not letting it go, then?" Sean said.

"You don't know that," I said.

"Michael, I know that. Just make sure she doesn't get suspicious," he said.

"Hard to do, don't you think?"

It was an open secret that my brothers and I were involved in organized crime. The hotel was completely clean. Patrick insisted it stay that way, but I had no illusions that everyone thought of the business as illegitimate and that included Eden.

"What people whisper about is not our concern. Just make sure they stay in line. Legally," Sean added.

"I will. Is that all?"

"You coming into Boiler Room tonight?"

"Maybe," I said, hesitating to commit because I wasn't sure when I would leave the hotel. "I need to look over the books."

Sean smiled. "Michael can't come out and play because he has to do his homework."

"Fuck off, Sean," I muttered, though there was

no real feeling behind the words. I did have home-work, and Sean was just breaking my balls, one of his favorite pastimes.

He punched me on the shoulder and left, not harping on the point like I knew he could have.

I appreciated the rare moment of mercy.

I was having a hard enough time reconciling this change, and not having to even deal with Sean's bullshit made it that much easier.

I trudged back up to the executive suite but wasn't in the mood for another go-round with Eden. So instead, I walked the hotel, keeping my eyes peeled for anything that might be out of order.

Though I would never admit it to anyone, least of all my brothers, doing so calmed me. The hotel ran like a well-oiled machine, and seeing it continue to do so made me proud.

Still, I knew this wasn't me.

I was a Murphy, not a hotelier, and no matter how much my brother wanted to make me into one, I never would be.

Still, I'd play his game, do as he asked, but soon, I would take my rightful place in the family.

And get the fuck away from Eden.

THREE

EDEN

A FEW HOURS LATER, I was happy when I found the employee break room empty. I could've gone to the office that I shared with Gerald but I needed a little time alone.

Time to decompress from my last go-round with Michael.

It sucked beyond belief that all these hours later, I was still shaken, still excited, but that was just the way it was with him, and I knew better than to try to pretend otherwise.

I sat at the table and sipped a glass of water as I flipped through a magazine, consciously forcing my mind not to think of Michael, the way his eyes lit, the always stormy expression on his face, how much I wanted to kiss his lips.

Nope, I didn't allow myself to think any of that, didn't allow myself to think of anything but how frustrating and irritating the man was.

I'm sure he thought the same of me, and while that hadn't been my intention, I wasn't sorry about it.

After the Murphys bought the hotel, Michael had come in with no consideration for what we'd built over the years. If he'd shown just an ounce of humility, some interest in understanding what it was we did, how the staff had kept the hotel running for years, I would have been more receptive, to make no mention of how appreciative I would have been if he'd tried to keep the peace with Gerald.

However, Michael Murphy didn't do peace and understanding, and he certainly didn't do humility. I'd felt compelled to step into the breach and provide a buffer between Michael and the rest of the staff, a role Patrick Murphy had more or less made official.

A role that I loved, though I would never admit it.

Michael was exasperating, but he was also exhilarating, put some much-needed excitement in my orderly, but rather boring life.

"Eden?"

At the sound of Gerald's voice, I pushed aside thoughts of Michael and let a smile cross my face as Gerald approached.

I set down the magazine and then stood. Gerald stopped in front of me, always at a respectful distance, and put his hands behind his suit-clad back.

"Hello, Eden. I was wondering where you went," he said.

"I just came to hide out," I said, looking up at Gerald, smiling.

"I'm not surprised that was necessary," Gerald said. "You've spoken with Mr. Murphy today, I take it?"

As always, Gerald kept that same mild expression on his face, one that could mean anything. But I knew him, and I knew exactly what it meant.

Of all of us, Gerald had had the most trouble adjusting to Michael's presence. He pretended not to mind the change in ownership, did a pretty good job of it too, but I had known Gerald since I was nineteen years old.

I could see past his bland smiles, his extreme

politeness. Saw how deeply Michael's presence at the hotel hurt him.

Which was completely understandable.

I'd been at the hotel for more than a decade, but Gerald had been here much, much longer. He'd never owned it, but it had been his life's work, and the former owner, an elderly woman who had inherited it from her husband, had left it to Gerald to run as he saw fit.

So her sale to the Murphys, and the corresponding renovations had been a shock to us all, none more than Gerald.

We'd always worked hard to maintain the hotel, but it had been a budget-friendly place that catered to working families and travelers looking for an inexpensive stay in the city. Gerald had always treated it and our guests with the utmost integrity, but the adjustment from budget hotel to high-end, exclusive, cutting-edge hotspot had been a challenge for him.

I tried my best to paper over it, make sure that he and Michael and the rest of the Murphys didn't have occasion to cross paths. Still, I felt for him. He'd poured his heart and soul into this place, and as much as I might try to pretend otherwise, as much as he might try to, it had never been his and never would be.

"It's fine," I said, smiling at him as brightly as I could, never sharing with Gerald the full nature of my conversations with Michael.

Gerald didn't look convinced, and I thought he looked concerned. But that was one area that always left me off balance.

I'd known him for a very long time, and he'd taught me so much about the hotel industry, but our relationship had never gone deeper, certainly not deep enough for me to say with surety he was concerned. It was funny, because I thought I was close to Gerald, thought he felt the same way, but there was still always this lingering formality between us.

Probably his attempt to enforce the chain of command. Gerald was big on that, liked to have his rules and systems in place, and that was fine by me.

He'd always been a good general manager, fair and direct, so what could be viewed as his eccentricities never bothered me at all.

Plus, compared to Michael, he was a damn teddy bear.

"Did Mr. Murphy find fault with something?" Gerald asked, probing, not at all subtle.

Despite myself, I laughed, and the usually reserved Gerald cracked a smile. The question was funny, because Mr. Murphy always found fault with something, or someone, usually me.

"He had some questions about personnel," I said, being vague.

"And you weren't amenable to those questions?" Gerald said.

I paused, considering Gerald's question and my response. I decided to continue to be vague, not necessarily wanting to feed rumors, not that Gerald would engage in that sort of thing.

"Let's just say we couldn't reach a mutually satis-factory conclusion," I said.

Gerald smiled. "I taught you well."

I laughed but then went silent as Gerald studied me.

"What?" I said.

"The staff—I—appreciate what you do, Eden," he said, and then he cleared his throat.

I smiled again, feeling comforted at Gerald's rare expression of gratitude.

"It's no problem. I've had a couple people look after me over the years, so I'm happy to repay the favor," I said.

"Well," he said, "be assured your actions are appreciated."

Gerald shifted uncomfortably and began adjusting the cuffs of his stark-white shirt. His skin, however, had flushed deeply, and it was clear that even that small display of emotion made him uncomfortable.

It was endearing, amusing, but I wouldn't dare laugh. Because what I said was true. People—Gerald—had given me a shot, and I had made it my mission to do the same for others.

Despite Michael Murphy's efforts.

"Be careful," Gerald said.

The sound of his voice made me realize I had drifted off, again caught up in thoughts of Michael. I looked up at Gerald, frowned when I saw his intent look.

"Is something wrong?" I asked, concerned at his expression.

He gave the ghost of a smile, but then shook his head. "With Mr. Murphy." He cleared his throat. "I mean with Mr. Murphy," he said.

"Be careful?" I asked.

"You're a lovely girl, Eden. True and kind. Probably not used to people like him," Gerald said.

"And you are, Gerald?" I said.

He smiled briefly, but the look in his eyes didn't change. "I'm an old man. I've seen a lot. Be careful with him. He's dangerous."

I shook my head. "He's a hard-ass, but he's not dangerous, Gerald."

I left the "at least not to me" unsaid. Michael would never hurt me, but whether that courtesy extended to others was something I dared not consider too closely.

"Whatever you say, dear," Gerald said indulgently. A moment later, his expression was the same neutral reserve that I had become so accustomed to seeing from him. "I'm going to do the rounds."

He left without saying anything else, and though I had my own tasks to get back to, I didn't follow, not immediately.

Something about Gerald's warning stuck with me, made me think more than it should have. It was no secret Gerald was not a fan of Michael's, and that the feeling was mutual.

It also wasn't a secret, at least as far as I was concerned, that the Murphy brothers were into some interesting business.

I somehow suspected that hotel linen and a marketing budget was not at the top of the agenda at corporate meetings among the Murphy brothers.

In fact, their reputations were well-known. I was a workaholic with absolutely no ties to anything as interesting as organized crime, but even I had heard of them.

I was ambivalent about the whole thing, or, more accurately, the *alleged* thing.

Michael's brother Patrick, the one who was ultimately in charge, had always been decent and fair. Even, occasionally, pleasant, something I couldn't really say for his brother. He treated the staff well, made sure they were compensated well, and gave Gerald and me, with the exception of Michael's presence, space to run the hotel.

Nothing else mattered to me, so I paid the gossip no mind.

Of course, that didn't change the truth of what Gerald had said.

Michael was dangerous.

I knew that, just as much as I knew anything else. Despite that awareness, I wasn't afraid of him.

Was annoyed by him, was, as much as it pained me to admit, powerfully attracted to him. But I had nothing to fear from him.

None of us did.

Maybe I should find Gerald, tell him that.

I considered it but then disregarded the idea.

Michael Murphy didn't need me to champion him—I had a million better things to do with my time.

I finished my bottle of water, closed the magazine, and then began my rounds, determined to keep Michael Murphy completely out of my mind.

FOUR

MICHAEL

HOURS LATER, after I finally left the hotel and drove to my brother Sean's pub and personal clubhouse, Boiler Room Irish Pub and Bakery, I was still replaying that incident with Eden over and over in my mind.

I didn't like that, didn't like it one bit, but in the sanctuary of my car, I could admit I was somewhat impressed.

Grown men didn't look me in the eye, let alone tell me no, but Eden had no problem with it at all. Seemed to relish doing so in fact.

When I was younger, I wouldn't have been able to tolerate that, accept her blatant disobedience.

I could barely tolerate it now but there was something thrilling about it.

About her.

Which made no sense at all.

She was, if I was being my most generous, cute at best. Her face was understated pretty and her curvy body looked soft, inviting, but I saw women more beautiful than her on an hourly basis.

None of them stayed in my mind for longer than a second, if that.

But Eden, Eden was nearby in my thoughts.

I'd understand if it was simply anger, me trying to figure out a way to neutralize her influence, get her to see that it would be in her best interest to cooperate with me.

That kind of focus, obsession, really, was something that was comfortable to me and something that was familiar.

But this thing with Eden wasn't.

Because I wasn't thinking about ways to make her comply, ways to get rid of her altogether if it came to it.

No, instead I thought about the way she so openly defied me, how much that turned me on, thought about how much fun it would be to turn the tables, have her under me, at my mercy, begging for more.

Something that was doubly frustrating because it wouldn't happen.

It would be a terrible idea for me because I wasn't going to mess this up. I wouldn't give Patrick a reason not to trust me and screwing Eden would be a very good one.

It wouldn't happen because I aggravated Eden as much as she did me. And she had given no hint that anger was only a mask for obsessive desire.

So, as much as I might want her, might be frustrated with her, there was no way around either, so I'd have to do my best to make nice.

I almost choked on the very thought.

I fucking hated making nice, had almost no experience with it.

But Patrick was insistent that I learn how to work within the confines of a legitimate business, that I couldn't just bend people to my will using whatever means were necessary.

It seemed that Eden was my test.

She was proving quite the challenge.

Still, I had to be careful, make sure that I didn't focus on her to the exclusion of everything else. As fascinating as this little game with Eden was, I had a hotel to run. Or a hotel to try to run. Between Eden defying me at every turn, Gerald Collins slinking around behind me, I had a lot to contend with. I wasn't worried.

I was determined to do this, determined to show Patrick that not only could he trust me, but that I could do what it took to improve our family's fortunes, even if it was something I didn't want to do. Once I did, he would allow me to take my rightful place.

Neither Eden, nor Gerald, would stand in the way of that.

Because once that happened, I finally, after all these years, decades, would have proven myself. And I wanted that more than anything at all.

I parked outside the pub and made my way inside. We sometimes used it to clean a small amount of cash, but it was mostly legit, a place for us and the neighborhood to hang out and the perfect environment for Sean to hold court and chase after women, something he seemed to have endless energy for.

It was one of the few places I felt completely comfortable, and looked forward to being there and hanging out with my brothers.

I saw Patrick's car, and got out, eager to see him.

He had been so preoccupied with his new bride, Nya, we hadn't seen him as much as we had before.

I was still struggling with that. I was happy for Pat, thought Nya was cool but I missed my brother. Sean said that I wasn't losing a brother but was gaining a sister, but I wasn't convinced.

Nya was nice enough, a good match for Patrick, but it had been just the four of us for so long, it was hard to accept another person's presence. Yet as I saw how happy Patrick was now, I sucked it up and kept my feelings to myself.

If anyone deserved it, Patrick did and I wouldn't do anything to mess it up. After pausing long enough to take off my tie, I headed into the bar.

It was still early yet, so the crowd was sparse, and I saw Sean immediately.

"Hey, Gracie," I called to the pub manager and head baker who was pretty much attached to Sean at all times.

"Michael," she replied without really looking up. I didn't mind. That shyness was just Grace.

"Just water today," I said.

She nodded and then quickly slid a glass across the bar.

"No tie, and you're drinking water?" Sean said.

"Some of us have to be responsible," I said,

taking a sip and pointedly ignoring the comment about the tie.

Sean smirked. "You sound like Patrick," he said.

I frowned at him. Sounding like Patrick was not something either of us ever wanted to do, but I ignored that and instead found Patrick sitting at the back of the pub. I walked toward him.

"Nya sick of you already?" I asked as I sat across the table from him.

"Never," he said as he took a sip of his whiskey. "She and her friend Jade are doing some woman thing, which means I'm stuck with you assholes. Quite the downgrade."

I laughed quickly, then looked at him, really studying him.

"What?" he asked.

"It's just…you look good, Pat. Happy."

I went quiet then, unaccustomed to expressing that kind of emotion.

"I am, Michael. Thank you," he said. "But enough of that."

"Agreed," I replied, smiling.

We moved on to other topics, mostly Patrick regaling me with stories of his bride and how much he loved her, his favorite topic at the moment.

I didn't begrudge him his happiness, but I

would be lying if I said it wasn't a little bit weird. None of my brothers expressed emotion freely, and to see Patrick like this, happy, looking as free as I could recall seeing him, made me happy.

Instantly I thought of Eden, but then quickly forced that way. What Patrick had with Nya was real. This thing with Eden was simply a battle of wills, one I was intent on winning.

"What has she done now?" Patrick asked.

I looked up, not having realized I had dropped my head.

"You haven't heard a word I said," Patrick stated, ending on a little chuckle.

"Of course I have. You're talking about Nya. How much you love her. How perfect she is. How perfect your life is."

Instead of being insulted by the somewhat testy tone of the words, Patrick laughed out loud.

"It was something like that, but you didn't hear it. And when you're this distracted I know there's only one cause," he said.

I twisted my face into a scowl. "What the fuck are you talking about, Patrick?"

"Oh yeah, it's definitely her," Patrick said.

"Who the hell is 'her'?" I said.

"Right, Michael," he replied, a knowing smile playing on his face.

I knew exactly who the "her" was, and I knew he knew it too. Quite irritating to have two of my brothers bring up the same topic with me on the same day. It was also a sign I needed to do a better job of hiding my thoughts. I didn't like the idea of anyone knowing what I was thinking, though with my brothers, such a worry was futile. What I liked even less, though, was knowing that Eden was the cause.

I needed to make sure she stayed out of my mind.

Starting now.

I looked at the door and watched as Declan, my second oldest brother entered. He nodded at Sean and didn't look at Grace. As he approached the table, he didn't slow and as one, Patrick and I stood, Sean behind us.

When we got to the back room, the air became even lighter, more relaxed.

We all loved Boiler Room, felt as comfortable there as we possibly could anywhere, but there was something about the four of us together that couldn't be replicated, and when we were alone, there was a freedom that we seldom felt in the presence of others.

"How is everything?" Declan asked.

"Bar's running fine," Sean said.

"And Aengus?" Patrick asked, this time looking at Declan.

"Still a scoundrel, but apparently taking a break for now," he said.

Patrick's expression was passive but I knew what he thought. We all hated our father, Aengus, but we'd all promised our mother he wouldn't come to harm at our hands. It was a promise we'd all kept so far, one that we still intended to keep, but despite it, after what had happened with Patrick and Nya, we resolved to keep a close eye on him. If he stepped out of line, the mercy he didn't deserve would end sooner than he thought. Something that wouldn't bother me a bit.

Until then, we'd keep an eye on him so we didn't get caught flat-footed.

"The hotel," Patrick said, looking at me now.

"Running smoothly. But it would be a lot smoother if you'd just put me in charge," I said.

"You are in charge," Patrick replied.

"But I have to ask permission every time I want

to fire somebody. Does that sound like I'm in charge to you?" I said.

I ignored Sean, who looked back and forth between Patrick and me, didn't look at Declan, who I knew had no reaction at all, and instead focused on Patrick.

"I gave Eden that responsibility to help you," Patrick said.

"And how is having to ask her permission before I can take a fucking piss helping me?" I said, allowing far too much of my frustration to show through. I knew my brothers wouldn't miss that, and that Sean especially was filing my little outburst away for later use.

Patrick frowned, then took a deep breath. I could tell I was testing his patience but I didn't care. "It helps because you don't want to alienate the staff."

"I don't give two shits about alienating staff," I shot back.

"My point exactly. Eden's got a cool head on her shoulders. Everybody likes and respects her. Plus, she's got the balls to stand up to you. Which makes her perfect for the job," Patrick said.

"Pat, this is bullshit. If you want me to run the fucking hotel, give me the power to do it," I said.

"Michael, if you want to run the hotel, prove to me that you're capable of doing so," Patrick shot back.

And that was the end of that conversation. I had known that I shouldn't bring it up, but I hadn't been able to help myself.

I was sick of being coddled, of Patrick not respecting me. Hated it, in fact. For as long as I could remember, I'd done what he asked, tried to prove each and every day that I was worthy of my name, of being his brother.

So far, at least, I had failed.

He'd never said as much, at least not directly, but he had made it clear in his actions, in the way he never trusted me to do anything of value. He tried to play it off as teaching me how to manage in the underworld and in the legit world, but I saw right through his bullshit.

He didn't trust me, and I wouldn't rest until he did.

But confronting him this way wasn't going to help. I had known that, had told myself that I was going to keep my mouth closed, not say anything, I hadn't been able to.

Eden wasn't even here and she was about to give me an aneurysm.

"Is everything else okay?" Patrick asked.

"It's fine. I plan to get rid of those two security guards as soon as Eden says it's okay," I said sarcastically.

Patrick just smiled. "Well, I hope you can convince her."

I didn't respond to that and instead continued, "Things are quiet. None of the guests have been of note, and I haven't seen anything of concern."

"Good. I hope that shit has passed but keep your eyes open."

"Always," I said.

And it was true. We had navigated that particular threat to Patrick, but there were always others.

"Is there anything else?" Patrick said.

"No," I said.

"No," Sean said.

"No," Declan said.

"Good." Patrick stood. "Now let's go have a drink."

FIVE

EDEN

I WAS ready to end another grueling day and looked forward to putting this afternoon's excitement behind me.

Would have earlier if Michael hadn't lingered and if I hadn't been too cowardly to risk facing off with him again. So, rather than make a run to the employee parking area, I'd made myself scarce until I was certain he was gone.

Even now, I didn't go directly to my car like I should have. Instead, I made my way to the security office, curiosity I didn't quite understand taking me there.

As I walked toward the security office, I started

to fume again, remembering Michael's ridiculous request. Not firing those guards had been the right thing to do, especially since he refused to even give me some clue as to why they'd gotten on his bad side. If he couldn't give me at least some explanation, I wouldn't screw with those men's livelihoods because Michael Murphy had gotten up on the wrong side of the bed.

They had worked the late night and early morning shift for years, and there had never been trouble. Whatever Michael's problem, I knew it was nothing about the quality of their work, but checking in wouldn't hurt.

I swiped my access card, listened to the magnetic lock click as the door opened, and then went inside. I knocked on the metal door that separated the restricted area from the control room with the bank of cameras where Steve and Bob sat during the night and opened it.

Or rather, tried to open it. Couldn't because the door was locked.

I frowned, turned the knob again to confirm it was locked.

I reached for my keys, not exactly concerned, but knowing full well this was out of the ordinary. City regulations made it clear that the door was to be unlocked at all times, something Steve and Bob knew.

In the past, the staff hadn't always followed those rules, but when the Murphys had taken over, they'd insisted that every regulation be followed to the letter. Most staff that was still around had gotten with the program, but I knew old habits were sometimes hard to break.

Thankfully I kept my keys handy, even after I'd clocked out. I unlocked the door, pushed it open, and frowned in confusion at the empty room that greeted me.

The bank of screens on the wall showed scenes from the hotel, a steady image of the lobby and elevators along with a screen that rotated between the floors. The three chairs were empty.

During the week, there were only two guards, with a third working the weekend shift when the lounge was busiest.

Tonight, though, there was no one.

A locked door could be overlooked, but this…

I swore under my breath and then walked to the control panel and reviewed the last several hours of recordings as quickly as I could.

When I was certain there was nothing of concern, I grabbed my walkie-talkie.

Gerald was gone for the evening, so I radioed the night manager and let him know where I was.

Then I sat, stewing.

Michael would never let me forget this. I could picture him now, see the self-satisfied smirk on his perfect face, the equally self-satisfied glint in his eyes, both because he'd gotten his way and because I didn't have a leg to stand on.

I wasn't sure which would make him happier, but I had no doubt he'd be overjoyed.

I'd gone to bat for those men, and now I'd never live it down.

Which was bad enough but not something I would ordinarily take to heart in usual circumstances.

These were not usual circumstances.

Because after I handled this, I'd have no choice but to tell Michael.

Again I imagined how he would react, could practically see the smug smile he'd give me before his expression dropped back into its standard chilly reserve.

I was *so* not looking forward to that, but Steve and Bob gave me three long hours in the camera room to think about it. By the time they arrived, I was ready to boil over.

"Hey!" Steve, the guard who had worked at the hotel for over a decade, called as he entered the room.

One look at me, and this momentary exuberance faded. I'd never thought of myself as an intimidating person, and I doubted the last few hours had changed that, but between my unmistakable level of pissed off and Steve's awareness that he had been caught, whatever friendliness that had existed between us was gone.

"Eden, I—"

I held up my hand and shook my head. "Bob's coming, right?" I asked, not even attempting to hide my displeasure.

"He'll be here in half an hour," Steve answered.

"Then sit. We'll wait for him to arrive."

I took the chair I had only just vacated, certain that at any moment my temple would start to throb.

There would have been no explanation they could have given for not being here, but this was even worse than I had thought.

It wasn't unheard of, especially for those on the night shift, to slip away for an hour or two and overlap a couple of jobs. But this kind of blatant activity that disregarded the safety of our guests, to make no mention of making me look like a fool, could not be tolerated.

"Why's the door open, Steve?"

Bob went quiet when he entered and saw me sitting there. Neither he nor Steve had their customary lunchboxes and thermoses, which told me they had clocked in and then left.

"Where are you working?" I asked, looking from one of them to the other.

"Eden, it's not—"

As I had done with Steve, I shook my head at Bob's protest. "All I want to hear are your answers to my questions," I said firmly.

Steve lowered his eyes, his face flushing with what I hoped was embarrassment. "Nowhere steady, and not always," he whispered. "This is just a little side thing."

"So you don't do this all the time is what you're telling me?" I asked.

He nodded emphatically and smiled. "Exactly. Sometimes there's just a little overlap. But it's nothing."

"Nothing?" I said, my voice rising. "You consider the safety of our guests and the people who work here, people who care about you, nothing?"

I was almost shaking with anger, but I fought to keep my cool.

"You know nothing happens here. Not since…"

"Not since what?" I snapped, my temper getting away from me momentarily.

"You know who owns this hotel," Bob said as I turned to look at him. "Nothing is going to happen here, so is it so bad that we wanted to make a few extra dollars?"

I knew exactly what Bob was alluding to, and knew he had a point. Even I took some comfort in the fact that the Murphys' reputation gave us some measure of protection. Guests were seldom as rude as they had been before and there'd been no violence since they had taken over. Still, I was furious.

"And what if something had? What if that fire a few months ago had been real? What if a guest had gotten out of hand with Gerald or Trudy in house-keeping?" I asked, knowing that Trudy in particular, given her advanced age, would strike a chord.

They both had the decency to look embarrassed, but I was beyond the point of caring.

"I guess you know you won't be getting your two weeks," I said.

"Yeah, but we can finish the shift," Steve said,

looking hopeful, probably thinking that if I gave on this, he'd be able to convince me to change my mind altogether.

Their shift was almost over, but I chose not to point that out. "That won't be necessary. I'll get the termination papers started and see that you get your checks for whatever pay is owed to you," I said.

Steve's eyes flashed, first with surprise, then with anger.

When I finally saw resignation, I stood, smoothed my skirt, and walked toward the door. When I reached it, I saw that the morning crew, who I had called to come in early, was waiting outside.

"Gentlemen," I said, nodding at them as I walked past.

I saw the curiosity on their faces, but didn't address their unspoken questions. We'd make an announcement tomorrow, but for now, I wanted to finish this business and finally go home.

During the grim ride down to the executive suite, I tried to keep my mind clear and focused, while Steve and Bob looked at me, eyes just this short of pleading.

Even if they tried, those pleas would have fallen on deaf ears. There was nothing to do now but finish this. Dismissal was my least favorite part of the job, but I knew the process well and had their termination papers prepared in half an hour.

I wrote a quick email to Gerald and left shortly thereafter, my gut twisting as I resigned myself to informing Michael.

SIX

MICHAEL

THE NEXT DAY, I entered the hotel with an extra spring in my step.

"Good morning," I said to the front desk agent.

The woman looked like she was going to faint, but then nodded quickly.

"Good morning, Mr. Murphy," she said tentatively, adding a little smile to the end of the words.

I kept going, considering her puzzled reaction but then quickly forgetting it. This morning, I couldn't think of anything except Eden.

And my victory.

I wondered if she knew that I knew, then determined she probably did.

Eden was no dummy, so she knew that very little happened in my hotel without me knowing about it. So her firing the guards after our contentious conversation definitely would not escape my notice.

She'd have to come and tell me that, and now I also had a chance to show Patrick I had done as he asked and managed the situation.

Of course, the fact that all of this had happened through no action on my part took away some of the shine, but only a little. I wasn't a stickler for rules. I cared more about results, and in this case, like always, I had gotten what I wanted.

I checked my watch as I passed the general manager's office, a little surprised when I found it empty. Eden was always here by this hour, so I assumed she was hiding out. I didn't like that, but I wouldn't push the issue. She'd come to me when she was ready, so there was no need to rush.

I sat behind my desk and waited.

Four hours later, my patience was completely shot.

I'd barely moved all morning, certain that at any second Eden would arrive.

That anticipation, every sound drawing my eyes toward the door expecting her, had taken what was left of my good mood from the morning and ripped it to shreds.

That was probably intentional on her part. After all, she knew how to get under my skin almost as well as Sean, and she knew making me wait would drive me nuts.

A smart tactical decision on her part, I decided, but one that still pissed me off.

This hotel might be her own personal crusade, but she was also my employee, and the happenings in my establishment merited my review. I'd tell her just that as soon as I found her.

I stood and walked toward the door, my anger brewing.

I pulled it open, but stood frozen when I saw Eden on the other side, her hand lifted as though she had planned to knock.

After I swung the door open, her eyes widened, and she dropped her hand, an embarrassed smile that was shockingly cute covering her face.

Seeing it made me want to smile back, an unfamiliar impulse, one that I ignored.

"Are you coming to see me?" I said gruffly.

That smile was gone in an instant.

"Yes," she said, her brows lifted, "which is why I was preparing to knock on the door."

"It's about time you showed up. Come in," I said.

I turned abruptly and walked back to my desk, trying to bring myself back under control.

Instead of sitting, I stayed standing, only a few inches away from the chair that faced my desk.

Eden didn't sit either and instead stood next to the chair, facing me.

I was much taller than her, but she didn't seem perturbed by that. Still, I could see that while she was dressed as usual, her jacket emblazoned with the M. emblem, her knee-length skirt neat and pressed, she was a little frayed around the edges.

I frowned as I studied her, not liking to see her like that and feeling an insistent need to know what was wrong and an even more insistent need to fix it.

"Why do you look like that?" I asked.

She frowned, stood stiffly, as if offended.

"Like what?" she asked.

"Like…" I looked her up and down, "that," I replied.

"Well, I'm not entirely certain what 'that' is, Mr. Murphy, but I had a very long evening, as I'm sure you know," she said stiffly.

If I wasn't mistaken, she looked a little hurt. Strange, especially since Eden was usually only

angry or exasperated when she talked to me, but I
ignored that and the fact I'd cared so much, and
refocused on the matter at hand.

"No, I don't know anything. Is there something
you want to tell me?" I said.

She smiled quickly, but dropped the expression,
and I could see that she had agreed with at least the
first sentence.

I ignored the little spike of anger and looked at
her expectantly.

"Well, I had a very long evening because I had
to let a couple of employees go," she said.

"Really? Who?" I asked, feigning ignorance as
she so often did, enjoying having the tables turned
for once.

She narrowed her eyes at me, her gaze burning,
which gave me a sense of satisfaction.

"The evening security guards, Steve and Bob,"
she said.

"Really? The two I asked you to fire?"

She nodded stiffly.

"And what finally made you see reason?" I
asked.

She thinned her full lips, her eyes staring
daggers at me. When she spoke, her voice was tight.

"I received some new information and it changed my decision."

"What information?" I asked.

My tone had changed slightly, some of the playfulness I was feeling gone. I needed whatever information she had. I also didn't like being in the dark, couldn't ever afford to be.

Eden frowned, but for one of the first times since I had known her, it wasn't directed at me.

"It seems that Steve and Bob weren't content with one position," she said.

"Meaning?" I asked.

"Meaning they were working elsewhere as well," she said, her expression darkening even further.

"We don't have any policies against that," I said, remembering how I had sought to make one, and how she had argued against it.

"No, we don't."

"So what's the problem?" I asked, starting to get pissed because this apparently went deeper than I'd first thought and even more pissed Eden had fought me on this. I wouldn't react until Eden explained, though.

"It seems that one, or both of them, would clock in and then leave to go to another job," she said.

"And leave my hotel unsecured?" I asked, leaning forward as the implication of what Eden said started to settle in.

Eden looked alternately angry and sad as she slowly nodded.

"I'm afraid so. When I discovered this information, I didn't see any other recourse but to let them go," she said.

She seemed genuinely upset about it, and I had the unexplained desire to comfort her.

I didn't.

Instead, I processed what she had told me, the facts immediately becoming clear.

That made a lot more sense. When an attempt had been made on Patrick's life, the hotel had been without security, which left him, Nya, Eden, and everyone else here at risk.

That kind of oversight could not go unchecked, and I'd make sure it didn't. Later, after I finished enjoying this moment.

I let my lips curl into a half smile, saw from the scowl that crossed her face that she noticed.

"I didn't realize you found hotel safety a matter of amusement, Mr. Murphy," she said.

"I don't, and I guarantee you this will be addressed. But I couldn't help but notice the irony of the situation, something I'm certain you didn't miss either," I said.

"I have no idea what you're talking about," she responded, the words petulant, and also unconvincing.

I stepped closer to her without quite realizing why and then began to smile.

"I think you do," I said.

"Oh really?" she responded blandly, though the volcanic explosion in her eyes revealed what she was really thinking and instantly had me hard as a rock.

"I'm very glad that you finally came to your senses," I said, ignoring the insistent desire to kiss her.

Eden, on the other hand, looked like she wanted to slap me, but instead she simply said, "I don't know what you're talking about. All I did was exactly what I was hired to do. I found the issue and saw to it that the issue was corrected. Nothing more," she said.

I smiled slowly this time. "Of course not. But there's something you should remember," I said.

She furrowed her brow, lifted it in question. I waited until she asked.

"And what's that?" she said grudgingly.

I leaned in, got close to her, closer than I had

ever been. She lifted her eyes to meet mine, and I could see her surprise and her curiosity. For once, I had her complete attention.

"That I assume respect. Demand obedience," I said, pausing for a moment before continuing. "And I always get what I want, Eden. Always."

Her eyes darkened as she processed my words, her face dropping in a deep frown.

Eden didn't bother to say anything as she turned on her heel and left.

SEVEN

EDEN

I was so mad, I could hardly see straight.

Mobster or not, boss or not, Michael Murphy should have been very glad I eschewed violence, because more than anything, I wanted to smack the shit out of him.

There had been so many levels of fucked up in that conversation.

I'd avoided him for the better part of the morning, not yet in a place where I could deal with what I knew would happen.

And I'd been right to stay away.

After too little sleep and way too much thinking, I hadn't been in the frame of mind to deal with Michael this morning.

This afternoon either.

Couldn't have been, not with the way his question still stung.

His little speech about always getting what he wanted, his snide, know-it-all routine as I'd told him about firing Steve and Bob had been grating, irritating. But that question...

Why did I look like that?

What the hell kind of question was that and what kind of asshole asked it?

The Michael Murphy kind, apparently.

Of course, it didn't help I didn't know whether I was more annoyed he had asked such an asinine and insulting question or by the fact I cared so much.

Besides, I reassured myself as I stared at the bathroom mirror, I didn't look so bad. A little tired, maybe, but that was no reason for Michael to look at me like I was roadkill.

Not that it should matter.

It *didn't* matter.

I told myself that more than once, but it didn't take away the sting of embarrassment. Or the hurt.

I shouldn't give a shit what Michael thought of me.

I *didn't* give a shit what Michael thought of me.

I mean, us mere mortals didn't roll out of bed looking like models who did side work as superheroes. Besides, my work wasn't about my looks or what Michael fucking Murphy thought about them. I did a damn good job, took care of my employees and guests, and I certainly didn't deserve Michael's bullshit.

My internal pep talk lifted me up for all of ten seconds.

Everything I'd said was true, but that truth didn't take away how I felt when I remembered that question.

I slumped my shoulders and turned to leave the bathroom.

Ridiculed and lectured by Michael. It was shaping up to be a banner day.

I went to Gerald's and my office and found Gerald waiting there. He looked at me expectantly.

"You shared that news with Mr. Murphy I take it?" he asked.

He frowned over the word "news," his own displeasure undeniable.

I'd told Gerald last night, but the news of Steve and Bob's termination had spread rapidly, and he'd been fending off questions from department heads all morning.

"Yeah," I said, plopping myself in my chair, not caring of Gerald's disapproving stare.

"You did the right thing," he said.

"I know," I replied, "I just hate that it was his idea first."

I looked at Gerald, realizing that I was telling him Michael had wanted them gone, something I hadn't mentioned the day before.

If Gerald noticed, he didn't say anything, and I didn't follow up.

Instead, he sat at his desk, and grabbed some papers, which I assumed were the termination documents.

"They should be ashamed of themselves," Gerald muttered.

"I agree," I said, but Gerald wasn't done.

"Leaving the staff and guests unattended like that. It's unforgivable. Though, I guess they would say they were simply following the example that gets set by the top," he said.

"What does that mean? I think we set an excellent example," I said, sputtering, both with surprise and offense.

Gerald smiled kindly. "Not you and me, dear," he said. "I was referring to them." He waved in the direction of Michael's office before he continued. "Whatever they are, we must conduct ourselves with integrity at all times. Just because they aren't bound by it doesn't mean that we should behave in the same manner."

"Gerald, I don't think this is an appropriate conversation," I said stiffly.

He looked momentarily surprised but then nodded quickly. "Of course not. I should take my own advice," he said.

I nodded but didn't say anything else. It wasn't uncommon for Gerald to talk about integrity, always hinting but never directly saying he thought the Murphys didn't have any.

Before today, I'd never directly contradicted him about this subject, held back out of respect for him. Even now I didn't.

Michael made me homicidal, but his brother Sean was funny and kind, and even the intimidating Declan had always been courteous. And Patrick had treated us all well, including Gerald.

I knew that I had finally been able to afford a house after they took over the hotel and offered me a promotion, and that the lives of the rest of the staff had seen some significant improvements.

Maybe all that was paid for with dirty money. I didn't know for sure, and honestly, I didn't care. The Murphys had made our lives better, and that was what mattered to me.

It was on the tip of my tongue to remind Gerald he cashed those integrity-less checks twice a month, but I held my words and tried to shift back to more important matters.

"We need to do a review," I said.

"Of?" he asked, looking at me now.

"All departments. If Steve and Bob are doing this, we don't know what else we might have overlooked," I said.

Gerald nodded. "That's probably for the best."

"You want to get the ball rolling?" I asked.

"Sure," he said.

I nodded. "Good. Start coming up with a plan, but don't talk to anyone yet," I said, standing.

"You're leaving?" Gerald asked.

"Yeah," I replied. "I have to find us new security guards."

———

MICHAEL

About a half hour after Eden left my office, I left the hotel.

I passed Gerald Collins as I left, only giving him a curt nod. He returned the gesture, but I could see how much it pained him.

He hated my fucking guts. He'd never say so out loud, but I had no doubt about that and suspected he had no problem sharing that dislike with others, including Eden. Her loyalty to Gerald would explain why Eden went out of her way to disagree with me, and I was certain Gerald went out of his way to nurture any tension.

I reminded myself that I couldn't have cared less. As frustrating as Eden was, she was smart and if she couldn't see through Gerald's bullshit, it wasn't my problem.

Besides, I was anxious to talk to my brothers about what I had discovered, but I was also thinking about that earlier conversation.

It had been nice to get Eden to see the error of her ways, make it clear to her that in all things I would ultimately be triumphant, but I was also bothered.

Something I didn't like, and didn't understand.

I had been right that she looked different, but her hurt at the question stuck with me. I'd assumed she'd stayed late at the hotel and would use that to explain her looking so weary, instead she'd looked wounded.

It wasn't something that would ordinarily catch my attention, but so much of my reaction to Eden was out of the ordinary, and it bothered me, almost as much as that hurt look on her face had.

I made it to Boiler Room in no time, and though the place wasn't open yet, I found Sean and Declan there as I'd known I would. After I entered, both followed me to the back room.

"Eden send you home early today?" Sean asked.

"Eden doesn't send me anywhere, Sean. But she did fire those guards," I said, ignoring his attempt to bait me.

Sean laughed. "What did you offer her? A car? A house? A year of silence?"

"She saw the error of her ways," I said, knowing I was giving an oversimplified explanation and not at all caring.

Even Declan laughed at that one. "I don't buy it," he said.

I smiled. "I didn't think you would, but I had to give it a shot. It turns out those asshole guards have been double-dipping," I said.

Declan narrowed his eyes. "You mean they were getting paid for work they didn't do?"

I nodded. "Yeah. They'd clock in and then go to other jobs."

"Leaving the hotel unattended," Sean added.

"Yes," I replied.

"Fuck," Sean said, looking angry, as did Declan. "We should put some of our people there."

"I agree, but Patrick says no, that we need to keep the business separate," I said.

"So we have to deal with this kind of shit instead?" Sean said.

I understood his frustration more than I could convey. I got what Patrick was trying to do and thought it was a good idea in most situations, but this was a special case, and I thought it was foolish of him to keep us from using all of our resources.

I also knew Patrick wouldn't change his mind.

"Yeah, we do, but maybe I should talk with those guards anyway," I said.

"Just talk?" Declan said.

"Just talk," I replied. "At least this ties up the last of the loose ends on that thing with Patrick."

"So you think that's closed?" Sean said.

"I think so," I responded.

"Is he going to take you off your leash now?" Sean asked.

I glared at him, but didn't argue because I didn't have a leg to stand on. I wanted Patrick to trust me, had done everything I could think of to prove that he could. But I didn't know if it was enough.

"Maybe," I finally said. "And at least I got the upper hand from Eden."

At that, Declan smiled. "I wouldn't count Eden out yet."

For some reason, I thought he was right.

EIGHT

EDEN

LATER THAT DAY, as I turned into an almost empty parking lot, I tried yet again to shake Michael's words, my reaction to them, and again didn't do a very good job.

I parked, got out and walked toward the modular building, trying my very best not to think of Michael. As I often did when I was flustered, nervous, or agitated, I adjusted my clothing, taking extra care to smooth down my skirt and adjust the button-down shirt that had gotten wrinkled under my jacket.

Even as I did, I knew Michael's question was the reason I was so focused on my clothes, but I couldn't shake the impulse, as much as I might have disliked it.

"Kevin, are you here?" I called as I knocked on the metal door, searching for signs of my former coworker and a man I considered a friend.

I heard something move behind it, and a few moments later, the door opened and Kevin Carson emerged, his eyes shining as he came toward me.

"Eden!"

Kevin shook my hand enthusiastically, then went forward to brush a kiss against my cheek, his neatly trimmed beard tickling my skin.

"You come to take me up on the offer?" he asked, his eyes twinkling.

"You don't waste much time, do you?" I asked, smiling at him, feeling flattered.

"Nope," he responded, the pause after telling me he was waiting for an answer.

"Sorry. This is business," I said, adding a little shrug at the end of my words.

"Don't be. I'll change your mind," he said.

He spoke with a certainty I knew was misplaced.

I had known Kevin for years now, even though I had often considered taking him up on the offer, I had never quite been able to.

He was a wonderful guy, and anyone would consider him a good catch, but I didn't feel that way about him, though his obvious interest was nice for my ego. I tried not to take advantage of that or lead him on, but like I'd told him, I was here for business.

"So what do you need?" he asked.

"I need some help with staff," I said.

"You moved on from M.?"

There was a wealth of meaning in that question, and I knew I couldn't avoid it.

Kevin owned a staffing company, one that specialized in security guards, and while I hadn't had much chance to work with him, my other colleagues assured me he had excellent staff.

I would have known it myself if Michael hadn't forbidden me from doing business with Kevin.

Neither of them had ever given me the full story, but I knew there was some measure of bad blood between them. Today however, I was in a pinch, and I knew I could rely on Kevin to supply good staff.

And getting to piss off Michael would be my own personal bonus.

"No. This would be for M.," I said.

As expected, Kevin frowned.

"I don't think that would be such a good idea, Eden," he said, his smile dropping, though I could still see the deep dimple in his cheek.

"Kevin, I need staff, good guys, and I know you have them. And you know I'll make sure you are paid what you deserve," I said.

Kevin turned serious, looked at me with deep regard.

"You know who you work for, don't you?" he asked.

"Look, I don't want to start anything. But if you—"

"I don't want to either, but I need to make sure I understand this and you do too," he said.

"I need security guards, and I know you can get them for me. There's nothing more to it than that," I said.

"And your employer?" he asked, his voice quiet.

I crossed my arms, noticed when Kevin's gaze strayed down to my chest. I was irritated that I instantly compared the way Kevin looked at me with the way Michael had, but I ignored it, kept my focus on business.

"Do you have the guys?" I asked.

Kevin studied me, seeming to consider.

"I guess if I made it contingent on you going out with me, that wouldn't work?"

"Nope," I said, trying to lighten the word with a smile but still certain there would be nothing more between us.

"Right," Kevin said, seeming to accept what I said, at least for now. "How many guys do you need?"

NINE

MICHAEL

I WAS STILL IRRITATED after I left Boiler Room, but when I looked at the clock, that irritation faded.

It was time for my monthly appointment, the least favorite thing in my life, the one I had no choice but to do.

It seemed impossible to think, but I'd rather have Eden driving me insane than do what I was about to do now.

I may as well get it over with.

As I drove, I tried to keep my mind blank, focus on the city streets, and then, as I got farther away, the greenery that surrounded me. Anything other than what awaited me at my destination.

When I stopped in front of the house, I didn't get out immediately. Instead I stayed in the car, looked at the pristine grounds, still impressed at how the owners managed to make this look like a grand home and not a mental institution.

However it may have looked, that didn't change what it was. Heart heavy, I got out of the car and made my way to the side entrance. I entered, walked down the long hallway that had been designed to look homey, welcoming. But even the carefully selected design couldn't hide the more institutional aspects of the hall, the plastic lamps, the nonslip flooring.

I paused, then turned and entered the good-sized day room.

I didn't go to her immediately, but instead watched her for a moment. Her red hair, which had always been bright was now streaked through with gray. She was focused on her hands, working on needlepoint. The intent look on her face reminded me of Sean. He was the only one of us who'd taken after her, gotten her lighter hair and green eyes.

The head nurse nodded at me, and after I

returned the nod, she walked over to her, patted her on the shoulder to get her attention.

"Maura, you have a visitor."

When my mother looked at the woman and then followed her finger to where she pointed at me, my heart broke yet again.

She looked at me with green eyes, bright, untroubled, opposite of the way they'd been throughout my childhood.

"Hello, young man. You came to visit me?" she asked, her brows drooping.

I walked toward her. "Yes," I said. "Is that okay?"

"Of course," she replied, nodding excitedly. "It's been so long since I've had one." She stuck her hand out. "You are?"

She looked at me, her expression pleasant, yet slightly confused, as though I was familiar but she couldn't quite place me.

I reached out and grabbed her hand softly with one of mine and patted the back of it, noticed how age had softened and thinned her skin.

"I'm Michael," I said, almost whispering.

"Michael?" she responded, brightening. "I have a little boy named Michael. He's eight now. He's going to be something special when he grows up."

I pulled my hand away, unable to bear touching her as I listened to her words. My chest squeezed tight, the emotion of being here and seeing her like this so intense, it physically hurt. I breathed out deep then sat next to her.

"You want to tell me about him?" I asked.

She looked at me skeptically. "Really? You want to hear about him?"

"I'd love to, Maura," I said.

I thought she would bounce out of her seat with her excitement. "Oh. He's the loveliest boy. So kind, gentle. Maybe too gentle," she said, looking wistful.

"What do you mean?" I asked.

"He has such a good soul. But his father…" She shook her head. "His father doesn't like that. I worry he's going to try to take it from him."

"I think he'll be okay," I said, trying to comfort her but knowing I never could.

"His brothers will look after him as best they can, but they're just kids," she said, her face dropping. "I wish…"

She trailed off and I patted her hand again. She looked at me, her eyes troubled. Then she leaned forward, whispered as though she was afraid of being overheard. "I love all my boys and I worry about them. But my Michael…I couldn't bear it if anything happened to him."

I smiled at her, tried to comfort her as best I could. "I think he'll be okay," I repeated, knowing it was a lie.

"You think so?" she asked, her eyes telling me how much she wanted to believe.

"I do," I said.

After that I stayed silent, hating that she still lived with that decades-old worry, hating that what she'd feared had already come to pass.

All these years and my mother still walked in the past, locked in her own mind, her only escape from the reality that was outside of it. I'd heard these words hundreds of times, and each time they hurt.

"Good-bye, Maura," I said a little while later. Then I kissed her on the cheek.

"Will you come visit again?" she asked.

"Yes," I responded.

She smiled, waved at me, and then lost herself in her needlepoint, seeming no different than she'd been before I'd arrived.

I left, not daring to linger, knowing that doing this was selfish and that my visits only caused her pain. That she seemed not to remember them was the only way I could justify coming here.

It was pathetic, but I needed to see her, tried to hold on to the Michael she'd loved, the one she'd always wanted me to be.

Instead of the man my father had made me.

———

MICHAEL

I was exhausted when I left my mother, but there was no way I'd go home and be alone with my thoughts.

I couldn't see my brothers either, because doing so would only make me more emotional. My thoughts turned to Eden, but I shoved them aside.

She would provide distraction, something I knew no one else could. But I was in no state to be around her, be around anyone at all.

So I went to work.

And not to the pristine hallways of M. Lounge and Hotel.

No, the way I felt required a return to who I really was.

I drove to the industrial park outside the city,

the fading sun giving the huge buildings an eerie look that perfectly matched my mood.

Years ago, this place had been abuzz with activity, but now it was silent. That didn't mean there was no work, though.

I stopped outside of a rusted chain-link fence that looked like a stiff breeze would blow it over. That had been Declan's idea; the entire place had been, and it was a damn good one. For years we'd had to handle business wherever we could, but once Patrick got the money, Declan convinced him to invest in property. Now, we owned several dozen and moved between them at random, which meant we had space and privacy to handle business.

I flashed my lights four times, waited a few seconds, and then began to drive as the gate started to slide open. I drove through it. The yard looked deserted with rusted-out, abandoned vehicles and scrap metal strewn everywhere.

Another of Declan's ideas.

When I reached a shed at the back of the property, I parked my car inside, looked around the yard, and when I was satisfied everything was as it should have been, I walked toward the large warehouse.

Only my brothers and I knew the code to open

the doors, and once I'd entered it, the doors opened and allowed me in.

The interior of the warehouse couldn't have been more different from the outside.

The shabby exterior held state of the art equipment, the polished concrete of the floor shining under the harsh neon lights. The men who worked didn't even look up as I approached, but Declan came over when he saw me.

"You're not on tonight," Declan said.

We took turns overseeing operations, and I was scheduled to handle next week's.

"No, but I'm here. I can take over," I said.

Declan looked at me, studying my face. He didn't push, though, and instead nodded. "It's all yours," he said.

I watched as he walked away, and once he was gone, I went deeper into the warehouse, looking over each of the stations.

It was a smooth setup, with two rows of a dozen tables all in a line. Each table had a crate of bills next to it and a cash machine on top. Once the cash was counted and wrapped, it went onto pallets where it stayed until it went out into the world, minus our forty percent cut, of course.

It was sometimes hard to reconcile this smooth,

efficient operation with what it once had been. It was even harder to reconcile the people who ran it with who they had been.

Declan handled the details, but this was Patrick's brain child. Sean did the books, and I…

What role did I have?

Before, the answer would have been easy.

In those early years, I'd been quite happy to handle the enforcement side of the business, eager to make sure anyone foolish enough to wonder would have no doubts about us. A necessary part of the business.

When Patrick had taken over my father's shitty protection business and expanded it into laundering, things had been rough. Cleaning cash was lucrative but made you a target.

I'd been instrumental in making sure everyone knew the Murphys were not to be fucked with, and it was a role I had relished. One that had given me a chance to prove that I was worthy of my name, of my brothers.

Now Patrick wanted me to be something different.

I didn't know if I could, but I would try.

I thought about how disgusted my father would be if he ever saw this place.

Aengus liked to think of himself as old school, would have said we were accountants not gangsters, called us pussies too afraid to get our hands dirty. Aengus, for all his bluster, wasn't savvy enough to see that what we did was just as illegal and ten times more dangerous than what he'd started.

That churning hate that always came up when I thought of him sparked again.

He was an asshole, a fool, and I knew that. I also couldn't quite escape the fear that he was right.

I knew he wasn't—he'd never been right about anything as far as I could tell. Despite that, I always wondered, knew that maintaining respect was essential, something we couldn't live without.

Patrick had been right to build the business. If we'd continued as Aengus had planned, well, I knew how that story would have ended. With me and my brothers, dead, in jail, or worse, nothings like Aengus.

Patrick growing the laundering, expanding out into legitimate business was his way of giving us a chance. Giving me a chance.

I wouldn't blow it.

I took a seat at one of the empty tables and began to count.

TEN

MICHAEL

THE NEXT MORNING, I was still restless, antsy.

It wasn't a surprise.

Seeing my mother always left me this way. Again, I questioned why I did it. I didn't know the answer, but I knew I would be back the next month like clockwork.

I'd probably be the only one.

Patrick, Declan, and Sean helped make sure she was in the best possible facility, but I was the only one who visited her regularly. The only one who hadn't been able to let her go.

Probably because, like my father always said, I was a weakling. Needed my mommy. Whatever the reason, I tortured myself with seeing her, tried to take solace in the fact that at least her mind was free.

Even though that knowledge comforted me, it still took time for me to recover from seeing her. After I visited her, I usually stayed away from the hotel, but this month I found myself headed toward it.

I wasn't sure why, or more accurately, I wasn't willing to acknowledge why.

Because I was still thinking of my mother, but I was thinking about Eden even more.

Which both annoyed and confused me.

So why, then, was I spending almost every moment thinking of her, driving to the hotel only because the need to see her was so great?

I sure as shit didn't know, but I had no doubt that I wouldn't feel right again until I saw her.

So I parked in my reserved spot, nodded at the employees as I made my way inside.

I took the long way, not because I was seeking out Eden, but because it was good to show my face, let it be known that I was here. That doing so would mean I would pass Eden and Gerald's office was simply a coincidence.

I kept my eyes directly ahead, didn't look left or right as I walked past it.

Then I heard a laugh, one that I instantly recognized as Eden's. Immediately, my mind conjured an image of her face, the way her eyes crinkled at the corner when she smiled, her full lips turning up, but ever so slightly, almost like she had a secret she didn't want to share.

I scowled, wondering how I had such intimate familiarity with Eden's smiles, especially considering that they were never directed at me.

I started to move a little faster, figuring that I had done what I intended to. She was here, and I should get to work.

"It was good to see you again, Eden."

I paused at the sound of a deep, male voice, one that sure as fuck didn't belong to Gerald. I cut left and opened the closed door, entering Eden's office without knocking.

When I opened the door, I locked eyes with Eden, saw that she was surprised, and, at least to my eye, looking a little guilty.

I didn't focus on her for long and instead looked at the man who sat next to her, his eyes locked on mine, his face set in a smile that was more like a smirk.

"What the fuck are you doing here?" I said.

I glared at Kevin, the years that had passed having done nothing to detract from our shared animosity. He was the former head of security at M. Lounge and Hotel, a position he'd held for exactly fourteen minutes after Patrick had bought the hotel.

Kevin had made it quite clear what he thought of my family, and continuing to work at the hotel would have been bad for my sanity and his health.

So why was he here now?

He stood and faced me, never taking his eyes from mine. Eden did too, and though I could see her from the corner of my eye, I kept my focus on Kevin, irritated that he was here, pissed beyond belief that Eden seemed so happy about it.

"Mr. Murphy," he said, managing to make my name sound like the vilest curse.

"Get the fuck out," I said.

"Michael!" Eden said, not quite yelling but her shock and irritation clear. I didn't give a shit about either. Eden had brought him here, probably to mess with me. It was working so she shouldn't expect me to be polite.

Kevin made no move to leave, so I stepped closer.

"You need help finding your way out?" I asked.

Kevin stood a little taller, his face flat now, his eyes narrowing. He looked like he wanted to try me, and I was more than ready to show him what a mistake that would be.

Finally, though, he dropped his eyes, shook his head. "No. That won't be necessary, *Mr. Murphy*."

He turned then, looked at Eden. "Let me know if those new guys don't work out. And if you need anything else, anything at all, you know where to find me," he said.

The way he spoke told me he wasn't referencing business. I looked at Eden then, partially to see her reaction to Kevin but mostly because I didn't want to pummel this asshole.

Kevin was spoiling for a fight, one I would be happy to give him. But that wouldn't help me get on Patrick's good side, and I wouldn't jeopardize that just for the satisfaction of shattering Kevin's jaw.

Patrick would be proud. I was definitely making progress.

Eden moved toward the door, her expression that courteous, professional one that she only broke long enough to give me a hard glare.

"I'm sure they'll be fine. Thank you for your help, Kevin," she said. "Let me walk you out."

"He knows the way," I interjected, looking at her and ignoring him.

She scowled but I held her gaze.

"It's okay. I'll call you later," Kevin said.

I still didn't look at him, but I knew he'd added that last just to piss me off. It did, but I didn't want to admit why.

Eden had a life outside of the hotel, or at least I thought she did. I'd never really investigated, but the thought of her taking calls from him or anyone else didn't sit well with me. She was still looking at me, and I could see the war raging in her eyes. She looked down, but didn't look at Kevin. "It's no trouble. I'll walk you out," she mumbled, the guilt in her voice the only thing that kept me sane.

"No she won't. Now get the fuck out of my hotel," I said.

Eden lifted her eyes and opened her mouth to speak, but before she did, I grabbed her hand and began walking toward my office.

After a second, she followed. I didn't have to be a genius to know she was pissed. Good, at least we had that in common.

I led her into my office and slammed the door behind her. I didn't let go of her hand, not immediately. Instead I stood there, staring down at her as she looked up at me, her eyes flashing fire.

I studied her face, her brows drawn together tight, her jaw clenched in anger. I imagined seeing her face intense like that, but not out of anger but instead passion as I made her come with my fingers, my tongue, my cock. Only stopped thinking of that long enough to puzzle over why this woman threw me so off balance.

"Michael, what the hell—"

She didn't have a chance to continue before I cut her words off with a kiss.

———

EDEN

One second, I was prepared to give Michael the tongue lashing of his life, and the next he was kissing me.

Before my mind could comprehend it, my body was overtaken with a flood of sensation.

Michael's lips against mine, hard, demanding, and at the same time gentle, coaxing.

His breath mingling with mine as we both exhaled sharply. His hand holding my face, keeping me still, though there was no chance I would move, would do anything at all to break this spell.

There was no other word to describe it. In an instant, Michael had me entranced, his scent enveloping me, the heat from his strong fingers burning my skin, stirring my blood.

I parted my lips, my body asking for what it needed before my mind could form a thought.

Michael heard that question, answered it instantly.

He stroked his tongue across my bottom lip, didn't give me time to recover before he moved to my mouth, stroking his tongue against mine.

The pleasing shock of tasting him energized me, and I reached for him, curling my fingers against his chest, feeling the thud of his heartbeat, the granite-like muscles that covered his body.

Part of me couldn't believe this was happening, but the rest of me didn't care if this was real, a dream, didn't care why it was happening. I was going to enjoy it, deal with the consequences later...

"Eden."

For a moment, I didn't know what was happening, but when I heard my name again, recognized the tinny sound of the walkie-talkie, I opened my eyes, jumped back quickly.

On instinct, I reached into my pocket for the walkie-talkie, my mind racing almost as fast as my heart.

"Eden."

It was Gerald's voice, and after hearing my name a third time I was finally able to respond.

I turned my back on Michael, unable to look at him, not knowing what I would do—what I would ask him to do—if I did.

"Gerald," I said into the walkie-talkie.

"Can you come to the lobby? I need your assistance," he said.

"I'll be there in a minute," I replied.

I hoped my voice didn't sound as winded, as scattered as I felt.

I put the walkie-talkie back in my pocket, my heart still booming. Even though I wasn't facing him, I was aware of Michael, my entire body was tuned to him, wanting to continue that kiss, take it further.

Wanting to understand why.

But despite what I wanted, my brain, which was miraculously still working, told me to keep moving.

I couldn't quite make myself move, though,

waiting for him to say something, afraid that he would.

More afraid that he wouldn't.

He didn't.

I waited one second, another, and then, finally, I left.

ELEVEN

MICHAEL

It had taken every ounce of willpower I had not to bring Eden back and finish what I'd started.

The only result that would have been satisfactory was me bending Eden over my desk and fucking her until neither of us could move. That realization hit me with stunning clarity, and that clarity froze me in place.

As quickly as I thought it, I knew that was the missing piece, the reason she so easily got to me.

On the surface, it didn't make sense. Eden was…Eden. I liked meekness, women who were content to be seen and not heard. And that wasn't Eden, not at all.

Even as I argued with myself, I knew the truth.

I wanted her. I just didn't know what I would do about it.

I'd been at the hotel for less than thirty minutes, but I left, knowing that if I saw Eden again, there was no way I'd be able to keep my control.

Still, we had matters to discuss, so as I drove, I dialed the number I knew by heart. I winced with irritation at how that number and everything else about Eden was always at the top of my mind and then pushed that thought aside and focused on the road.

Eden answered on the third ring. "M. Lounge and Hotel. This is the assistant general manager speaking."

She sounded so calm, not at all affected by that kiss as I had been.

"What the fuck was Kevin doing at my hotel, Eden?"

She sighed, sounding incredibly put-upon, something that would be amusing if it wasn't directed at me.

When she finally spoke, she sounded calm, patient, like an adult correcting an unruly child. "I'd really fucking appreciate it if you wouldn't fucking swear at me, Mr. Murphy."

Her words caused the most unexpected response.

I smiled, came dangerously close to laughing.

Ordinarily, I would have thought it cowardly to call her, but I was glad I had taken that approach. If she'd seen me smile, knew how close I was to laughing, it might make her think I wasn't serious. I was.

"Fine," I said, conceding the point. "What was Kevin doing in my hotel, Eden?"

"We've had a shortage of security personnel, and Kevin has the best contacts in the city. He's going to provide us contractors until we can work out a permanent solution," she said.

That smile from moments ago was now a distant memory. After that brief moment, Eden was doing that thing I hated, using that stiff, professional tone that made it seem like I was a stranger to be managed, not the man she would have let fuck her senseless.

It drove me nuts, made me want to demand the intimacy that we'd shared before. I wouldn't let it show, though. Eden seemed to be having no trouble keeping her emotions under wraps.

I would do the same, no matter how hard it was.

"You know how I feel about him," I said,

reminding myself Eden had provoked this but still trying to mimic the calm that seemed to come so easily to her.

"If I didn't before today, you certainly made it clear. And it's my hunch the feeling is mutual," she replied.

Eden's voice told me she thought Kevin was justified in his dislike, suggested that she took his side, something that threatened to further set me off.

"I don't fuc—I don't care how he feels. I don't want him in my hotel," I said, somehow managing to hold onto my control.

"Fine," Eden said on a sigh, "I'll make sure Kevin doesn't come to the hotel unless it's absolutely necessary. Of course it probably doesn't matter. I wouldn't be surprised if Kevin called his guys back."

"And upset you?" I said, my voice darkening. "No chance."

I was so tempted to probe, ask what their relationship was, but I didn't. I didn't want to care, but that wasn't what stopped me. No, the fear of what she might say stilled my tongue.

"Is there anything else, Mr. Murphy?" she asked.

"No."

I hung up the phone without saying good-bye. I'd hear about that, and in fact looked forward to Eden raising the topic of phone etiquette the next time I saw her. Or maybe she'd be direct, tell me that I was being a rude asshole.

I didn't know which, never knew how Eden would come at me. That was a part of the thrill.

Also, I realized I was in even deeper shit than I'd thought. Wanting to fuck her was one thing. Being desperate to talk to her was another thing altogether.

I parked my car, got out in front of the warehouse that had been converted to condos, ran up three flights of stairs, and pounded on the metal door.

"What the fuck!"

I heard Sean clearly through the door, laughed, knowing I'd woken him up. "Open the door, Sean!" I yelled.

A moment later, I heard the locks disengage. Sean opened the door a crack, just enough for me to see the sun glint off his beard and the silver .45 he held.

"Move, asshole," I said, pushing my way in.

He stepped aside to allow me entry and then

closed and locked the door. "You were going to shoot me?" I asked, turning to stare at him.

"I should. Why are you here so early?" he grumbled as he ambled across the open loft area to his platform bed. He put the gun on the nightstand and slid his glasses onto his face.

"It's nine thirty. That's not early," I said.

As a spoke, I walked to his neatly organized closet area and threw some workout clothes at him.

"Change," I said, lifting my own gym bag. "We're going for a run."

———

MICHAEL

"So, that was awesome," Sean said drolly when we returned to his apartment after a five-mile run.

"Glad you thought so. I was worried, especially since I had to practically carry your ass that last mile," I replied as I tossed him a bottle of water from the fridge and grabbed one for myself.

"I just didn't want you to feel bad. But, as *awesome* as that was, why the hell was I running at the crack of dawn?" Sean said.

"It wasn't dawn. And does it matter?" I asked.

Sean downed half his water in two quick gulps and then looked at me.

"I know I'm the most charming, most handsome, most intelligent of your brothers, but my peerless company is not the reason you dragged me out of my peaceful slumber to go running with you," he said.

"I'm just glad you were alone," I said.

"An oversight I intend to correct later this evening. But seriously, Michael, what's going on? Is it Mom?" he said.

His entire demeanor changed with the utterance of that single word. I knew she wasn't Sean's favorite topic. He had his own unresolved issues around her, so I shook my head quickly. "No. It's not," I said.

Sean's relief was palpable, but in the next breath, he looked at me, again curious. "So what then?" he asked.

"I didn't want to run by myself. I didn't expect that to lead to a fucking inquisition," I snapped.

Sean grinned. "It's Eden. She's on your ass again, huh?"

"Fuck off, Sean," I said, throwing my empty bottle at him.

He swatted it away effortlessly, grinning even bigger now.

"It's her. Tell me all about it," he said.

"Think what you want. I'm out of here," I said, heading toward the door.

"You're running away. That's definitely Eden. Come by the pub tonight and we'll talk it over," he said.

"Bye, Sean."

I slammed the metal door, still heard his laugh behind it.

TWELVE

EDEN

I found the most private seat in the lounge that I could and settled there.

It wasn't my habit to hang out here, and Gerald would have had a fit if he knew I was. He'd always preached that the facilities were for guests, not staff, that it was improper for us to use them.

Most times I would have agreed with him, but it had been a hell of a long day, and I needed a break.

I caught the bartender's eye, and he nodded, letting me know he'd be over when he had a free moment. Until then, I was content to sit, wait.

Stew in my own thoughts.

Michael had been furious about the guards. I'd intended that, something that embarrassed me to admit now that I wasn't in the throes of anger. That had been low on my part, but like always, Michael's reaction had been over the top.

That wasn't what was preoccupying me, though. Thinking about those moments, trying to interpret Michael's reaction left me stumped. As angry as he had been, I was positive, certain, he hadn't intended to kiss me.

But he had. If Gerald hadn't interrupted, he would have taken it further.

And I would have let him.

Even now, I shivered at the thought of that, not sure if the shiver was from pleasure, anger, or disdain. Maybe all of them.

I didn't even *like* Michael.

I tried to remind myself that over and over again. Believed it most of the time, too. But when he had been so close to me, kissing me, I'd been gone for him. Ready.

For years I had kept up with the outward illusion I wasn't attracted to him and had been able to keep that little secret to myself.

Not anymore.

I could try to pretend, play it off like I hadn't been two seconds away from begging Michael to fuck me, but that would be a waste of time. There was no way I could deny it.

A part of me thought I should be embarrassed about it, but I wasn't, at least not completely. Instead, I wondered what Michael would do about it, wondered how, if, he would try to use that revelation against me.

It was a fool's errand to try to get inside Michael Murphy's head, and in any case, I was vastly unqualified to do so, didn't know the man well enough to even begin to guess.

Still, my mind kept coming back to one nagging worry.

Had that kiss been strategic, designed to gain something that had nothing to do with me or any feelings he might have for me?

I couldn't dismiss that out of hand, but I wasn't sure. Michael didn't strike me as cruel, and kissing me to shut me up would have been.

And that explanation didn't fit with what I had seen.

Michael had recovered from that kiss quickly, but he'd been affected.

I was certain of that. Which meant I needed to figure out what I was going to do next.

I didn't know, but a nice glass of whiskey would help me figure it out.

"You're drinking here tonight?" the bartender asked as he came over.

"Don't tell Gerald," I said.

He smiled, winked at me conspiratorially.

"What do you want?" he asked.

"A Balor," I responded, deciding if I was going to drink whiskey, it might as well be top-shelf.

"Heavy-duty," the bartender said, looking at me skeptically.

On those few occasions I drank, I seldom had anything stronger than a wine spritzer.

"I'm indulging a little," I said.

"Your secret is safe with me," he said, preparing to head back to the bar.

"Hold that," Sean Murphy said as he appeared, seemingly from nowhere.

He extended the bartender a fifty-dollar bill, but before he took it, he looked at me. I nodded, and he smiled, walked back to the bar. Once he was gone, I looked at Sean, curious as to what that was about.

"Sean," I said, nodding at him.

"You have the look," he said, studying me intensely, the dim light of the bar reflecting off his classes.

I tilted my head, wondering where Sean was headed with that. "Meaning?" I asked.

"Yeah, I recognize it. The I-want-to-kill-Michael-Murphy look," he said.

I didn't want to *kill* Michael Murphy, and that was my problem.

I looked at Sean, suspected he could gather as much if his knowing smirk was anything to go by. Then again, most of Sean's expressions tended toward smirks of various types, so I couldn't be sure if that was knowing or just his regular expression. I chose not to investigate that question too deeply and instead looked at him.

"Just kicking back after a long day," I said noncommittally.

Sean smiled. "I can count on one hand the number of times you've had a drink at the bar."

"You're not here every day," I said.

"And I'm an excellent judge of character. You need a drink, and not at a place like this," he said.

"'Place like this'? Aren't you a part owner?" I asked.

"Grab your bag, and let's go," he said, ignoring my question.

"Sean…" I said, looking at him skeptically.

"Yeah, I know. Protocol and all that. But let's

get out of here. I think you'll have a good time," he said.

I studied him, listened to the quiet tinkle of piano keys. Thought about how staying here would only make me think of Michael. Going off with his brother would probably do the same, but at least I'd have a good time. Sean was nothing if not amusing.

"Let's go," I said, standing.

———

EDEN

"That was…interesting," I said after Sean led me down a flight of stairs and into the interior of his pub.

"Live a little," he said.

"I survived that trip, which was more than enough for me," I said, smiling.

In truth, Sean was a little heavy on the gas pedal getting here, but I hadn't been too worried.

"So do I get a tour?" I asked.

I looked around the room and saw a couple dozen people who murmured quietly in seeming comfort.

Sean extended his hand and spun on his heels. "Eden, this is my pub. Tour's over," he said.

I laughed, then looked at Sean as he nodded at a young woman who hovered near the bar. "Hey, Gracie," he said in the woman's direction.

She hadn't looked up, but I got the impression she was deeply aware of Sean and that she was evaluating me.

She finally looked at Sean and gave him a slight smile. "Hi," she said.

If I hadn't been looking at her mouth move, I wouldn't have heard what she said, but when Sean smiled back at her, she beamed. An instant later, though, she lowered her eyes, resumed that stance that screamed she wanted to be invisible, and something about her touched me, made me want to take care of her.

"Come on," Sean said.

He reached for my hand and pulled me toward one of the tables.

I didn't make it one step before I felt another hand curl around my other wrist.

I hadn't looked back, but the tremble that went through me at the first touch, the excitement I felt at it, left no doubt as to who held me.

He growled, "What are you doing here?"

It was screwed up that hearing his gravelly

voice, the anger in it, reminded me of that kiss, but it did.

I paused a moment and then turned to look at him.

"Michael," I said.

"Eden," he replied, his dark eyes flashing.

Since I had seen him last, he had taken off the suit jacket, opened up three buttons at the neck of his shirt.

He looked devastating, and it was all I could do not to rub myself against him.

I didn't, though, and instead moved farther away from him when Sean dropped my hand.

"Michael," Sean said, the amusement clear in his voice, "how's it going?"

"Don't say shit, Sean," Michael barked.

I looked at Sean, who gave him a mock wounded look, which seemed to make Michael even angrier.

"I'll deal with you later," he said to Sean. Then he turned to me. "Come with me."

He turned, not bothering to wait for an answer, but I didn't move. After that kiss, everything I thought I knew about Michael had shifted. As had everything I thought about myself. He was angry, but that didn't worry me.

What worried me was what I would do if I was alone with him.

"I was about to have a drink with a friend of mine. If there's something you need to discuss with me, you can make an appointment," I said.

I heard the voices of the bar quiet, felt a little tremble in my chest at Michael's glare.

He stepped closer, so close that our bodies were touching. Then he glared down at me.

"Do I have to carry you?" he said seriously, but then, Michael was pretty much always serious. I just was in no mood to humor him.

I huffed, crossed my arms under my chest, and glared at him. I didn't care who he was, he was not going to push me around.

"I don't think you heard me. I'm here to—"

My last words died in a shriek when Michael lifted me.

I looked back at Sean, who was laughing uncontrollably.

I was fuming, but knew that trying to get out of Michael's arms would be futile.

But he'd hear about this.

He carried me across the entire pub floor and into a back room where he slammed the door.

He set me down and stared at me. I stared back at him, anger sparking in my blood.

"Michael, I don't know what the hell—"

His lips capturing mine swallowed the last of my words. I shouldn't have been caught off guard, not with the way he'd been looking at me, and when he kissed me, I followed instinct and opened my mouth to allow him in.

He wasted no time deepening the kiss, holding me so I was flat against him.

"Eden," he said when he broke off the kiss, his voice still gruff. I could feel the warmth of his breath against my face, the softness of his lips against the corner of my mouth.

"Michael," I responded. I intended to sound like he did, but instead my word was more of a beg, something I didn't like but couldn't hide.

Even Michael didn't sound like himself. I'd opened my eyes at the sound of his voice, hearing something in it that I didn't recognize.

There was frustration in his words, anger, but something else, something like longing.

It was hard for me to believe, and it shouldn't have been, not with his insistent hard-on prodding me, nor with the way he'd just kissed me.

Still, my mind boggled at the thought of Michael Murphy wanting me.

I felt compelled to speak, not sure what I would say. "I—"

"Shut up," he said.

Then he kissed me again, moving so quickly that I didn't have time to argue. And as I had before, I gave in to him, kissing him back feverishly, unable to do anything else.

He trailed his lips against my jaw and then said, "Whatever this is—"

Whatever he was going to say was lost to the hard bang on the door. I jumped, but Michael seemed unperturbed.

"Fuck off, Sean," he called without even turning.

I thought I heard a gruff laugh through the door, but I was so caught up in what Michael was doing to me, I couldn't be sure.

And didn't care.

Of their own volition, my fingers had reached for him, curled themselves tight around his fine woven shirt.

He looked at me now, face mere inches from mine.

"What do you do to me?" he said.

THIRTEEN

MICHAEL

I STARED AT EDEN, her lips pouty, wet from my kiss.

My own mind reeling, spinning, and all because of her.

I hadn't intended for her to hear it, but wanted an answer.

What did she do to me?

I had no idea, but I'd find out.

My thoughts were consumed with her, consumed *by* her, and I hated it.

There was little respite from thoughts of Eden, the way her eyes flashed when she looked at me, angrily but still passionate.

I simply needed to get her out of my system.

I'd do this, it would be over, and I could go back to hating her and having her do the same.

Except, some small voice in the back of my mind whispered, made me wonder if maybe, possibly, this would take more than once.

I couldn't countenance that thought, couldn't give any power to it.

Instead I reached for her and wasted no time pushing my hands up that prim little skirt.

It was amazing, her warm skin softer than the satin that covered it.

I reached between her thighs, smiled when she clenched them, trapping my hand against her.

Her underwear was already wet, telling me of her need, and it was one I intended to fill.

I stroked my finger against her, the feeling driving me insane.

Eden arched, rocking against my finger and let out a deep, breathy sigh when I pushed the seat of her panties aside and brushed my finger against her skin.

The first contact with her bare skin made me moan.

It shouldn't have surprised me, not with the way Eden managed to affect me, seemingly without effort. I did it again, questioning if one taste of her would be enough.

I'd make it so, determined I would get her out of my system, wouldn't let her get any deeper.

I pulled my hand away, saw her eyes flash when I did, but I didn't linger and instead pulled down her panties. After that kiss, I'd known it would come to this and had made sure I had condoms, something I was grateful for now.

I grabbed one from my pocket and then opened my pants and covered myself, smiling at the way Eden gnawed her lip between her teeth, looked at me with desire that almost matched my own.

She leaned back, sitting atop the desk without my encouragement, spreading her thighs in bold invitation.

I stepped between them, rocked my hips to prod at her core. When I locked eyes with hers, I almost lost myself and moved forward to kiss her, needing to do something to break the spell.

It didn't.

Her lips against mine, her heat against my cock sent my already frantic need for her into overdrive. I grabbed her ass, loving the way it filled my palms.

I pulled her closer, found her ready to accept me as I pushed inside her. I moved until there wasn't even a millimeter of space between us, Eden's thighs spread wide, her fingers curled against my chest, her warm, wet heat cradling me.

This was everything I had imagined, more than, and I closed my eyes against the power of the sensation, the power of her.

This wouldn't be enough. I knew that now, but couldn't allow myself to accept it.

So instead I moved, thrusting into her, lifted by her reaction, her moan, the way she kissed my neck, her fingers groping my chest in a silent plea for more.

Something I would give her.

I thrust hard, moving into her with a force that left me breathless.

"Michael," she whispered, her voice coming out heavy, her breath against my ear.

She pulled me tighter to her, clung to me, her arms wrapped around me.

My cock throbbed, going harder inside her.

I knew I wouldn't last much longer, but I held on as long as I could, reached between us to strum her clit. She arched again, tightened her fingers, tugging so hard the threads of my shirt stretched tight with the strength of her hold.

I anchored my arm around her waist, thrusting harder, wildly, almost frantic.

"Michael," she said again, her voice pleading.

I realized then I'd wanted this from Eden, suspected it was inevitable. Because Eden pressed against me, her breath against my ear as she pleaded for more was the definition of satisfaction.

Once wouldn't be enough.

Before I had time to process that thought, Eden sighed, her body going rigid as she cried out her climax.

It was beautiful. She was beautiful.

And her breath against my face, her walls clamping down to hold me, made it impossible for me to hold back.

I came, filling the condom while silently cursing that it came between us. I held Eden until my breath calmed, and then finally, reluctantly, pulled out of her.

She looked stunned, but then quickly moved, working hard not to meet my gaze as she searched for her panties.

"Looking for these?" I asked.

"Um, yeah," she said, reaching for them.

I lifted my arm, keeping them out of her reach.

"What are you doing, Michael?" she asked.

"I'll hold on to these. A memento," I said.

She frowned again, looking angry. I felt a deep sense of loss at the change in her, deciding I preferred the passionate Eden to the pissed one. But I didn't like the way she made me rethink everything, most especially how I felt about her.

I needed that to end.

I waited, watched as the war waged in her eyes. When I finally saw the coldness I'd come to expect, I nodded.

"Let's go," I said.

FOURTEEN

EDEN

I FOLLOWED Michael to his car, my legs moving on automatic pilot. I didn't look left or right, worried I might see Sean, but even more, trying to understand what had just happened.

Why I wanted it to happen again.

That encounter had been explosive, and even as I tried to process it, some part of me instinctively understood that Michael and I had been headed toward this moment for years. It had been more than I could have imagined, and, I feared, had unleashed a ravenous hunger that had me needy even after that shattering climax.

After I got into the car, I looked at Michael

quickly, and through the shadows, I could see his stony expression. But seeing that expression, knowing that Michael probably regretted sleeping with me didn't dampen my desire for him.

I wondered if anything would.

As he drove off, I looked out of the window, wondering what had come over me. I tried to muster some embarrassment, but found I couldn't. This would complicate things with Michael, but I couldn't bring myself to be sorry about it.

However, we'd need to talk about this, figure out what it meant.

I shifted in my seat and looked at him. "Michael, I—"

"Not now," he said without looking at me.

A surge of anger rushed through me, and I looked out the window again, struggling to hold my temper and somewhat amused that reality had so quickly reasserted itself. That was probably for the best. I could easily imagine letting myself think that sex had changed something, but Michael was still Michael, and I couldn't let myself forget that.

The ride to my house passed in silence, and it only occurred to me after we arrived that Michael knew my address. I didn't think about that though, and instead got out of the car the instant Michael stopped it.

To my surprise, he followed, but I still didn't speak. When we reached my front door, I stopped and looked at him, trying to figure out what to say.

When I met his eyes, I swallowed hard, the intensity in his expression making me shiver. After a breath, I spoke. "Michael, I—"

Once again he cut me off with a kiss, his lips commanding and coaxing and leaving me breathless. After my brain cleared, I opened my eyes and met his, the darkness of the blue, the intensity in them softened by something like tenderness. I lowered my lids, an attempted defense against that thought, one I knew I had no business even entertaining.

But I looked up again when Michael pulled the keys from my fingers, my animated mouse key ring looking so out of place in his large hand.

"You can come in anytime, Eden," he said.

It was only after he spoke that I realized he was inside while I stood outside, and I smiled at the irony of Michael inviting me into my own home. That smile dropped once I entered and he closed and locked the door behind me, then deposited the keys on the small table next to the door.

I studied his face as he took in my home, and then I started to speak. "Michael, I—"

"Where's your bedroom?" he asked, turning his eyes toward me, though I couldn't read the expression in them.

"My bedroom? Why?" I asked.

I realized the stupidity of the question when Michael tilted his head in that way that told me he was wondering if I was dense.

I chuckled lightly, suddenly nervous and also surprised. I wanted him badly, but I hadn't expected him to stay. Now that he was, this was taking on a new light. It was one thing to say I got caught up in the moment. But, this, this—now was a calculated choice, one I knew would have repercussions.

I looked at Michael. He didn't look patient, at least not exactly, but I could see that he was waiting, telling me without words the choice was mine.

As if there was a choice.

Moving with a boldness I didn't quite feel, I reached for his hand and began to walk, realizing that he had done much the same to me only a short while earlier. I walked toward my bedroom on shaky legs, my heart pounding with nerves, those feelings nothing in the face of my desire for him.

After we entered my room, I dropped his hand

and then stood still, looking at him as he looked at it. Then, moving with the same grace and ease that he always had, Michael walked to the small chair I kept in one corner and kicked his shoes off. His shirt came next, the shadowed darkness of my room doing nothing to hide the rippled planes of his chest, the ink of the tattoo I couldn't quite make out.

When he reached for his pants, I kicked off my own shoes but then stopped when he shook his head. "Don't take off your clothes," he said in that stern tone I said I hated but that had my sex clenching now.

I stilled and then watched as he removed the rest of his clothes, mesmerized as he opened a foil packet and slid it down his long, hard length.

I was breathless, on the verge just from watching him, and when he moved closer, his cock bobbing with each step, I knew it would only take a few of Michael's hard thrusts to send me over.

But when he stopped in front of me, he paused, staring down at me. And when he finally touched me, it was barely a graze of his fingers against my neck, down my padded collarbones to center his hands at the first button of my shirt. He opened the first, the second, third, moving slow, like there was no hurry at all, though I could see his own need.

He finished unbuttoning my shirt, and then he pushed it down and off my shoulders. But again, he moved slowly, letting his fingers play around the waistband of my skirt before moving them up my stomach and finally cupping my breasts in his hands.

I arched my back, moving without any thought other than Michael touching me. He stayed still, something I was powerless to do. Instead, I moved, the friction of my bra and his palm against my nipples making me cry out.

Near mindless, I reached for his wrists to hold him still as I arched my back deeper. But Michael being Michael, he didn't comply. Instead he pushed my arms back to my sides and then, after giving my breasts a hard squeeze, he unsnapped my bra and pulled it off. Did the same with my skirt.

Since Michael had kept my panties, I was naked and when I lifted my eyes to his, I shivered again, then stood on my tiptoes and pressed my lips against his collarbone, then stretched higher to kiss his jaw, then, finally his lips.

I brushed my mouth against his tentatively, then with more confidence, more still when he palmed my ass. I followed his lead and let my hands roam his body as I kissed him.

Again he broke away and stared down at me as if he was trying to figure me out. I understood the feeling. I had no idea what was happening here, either, but whatever it was, whatever the consequences, this felt right.

No longer content with simply kissing me, Michael pushed me back onto my bed. I gestured for him and he came, settling his big body between my thighs. His cock nudged at my opening, and I wanted him to thrust inside me, silently begged for him to do so.

He didn't.

Instead, after staring at me intently, he captured my lips and kissed me softly, tracing every inch of my mouth. He kissed me until I clung to him, limp, needy, desperate for him. Then finally he reached between us, stroking his finger along my wet slit. Apparently satisfied with what he found, he lined his cock up with my entrance and then filled me slowly until he was fully seated.

Then he stilled, rested his forehead against mine for a moment before he again kissed me. This kiss was even softer, gentle, something I never expected from Michael, something I didn't even know I had wanted from him.

Didn't know I needed.

That thought in my mind, I held Michael tighter as he drove me to ecstasy.

———

EDEN

As I'd ridden with Michael in tense, stony silence, I'd thought I would stay awake for hours, tossing and turning, wondering what the hell I had done.

After he left, I slept like a baby.

That was Michael's work.

He'd given me the most powerful orgasms of my life and then left, all with almost no words. I wanted him to stay but hadn't been brave enough to ask. So instead I'd let him leave. But rather than agonizing about what had happened, I'd fallen directly into bed and into a deep sleep.

Not surprisingly, the next morning, Michael was the first thing on my mind.

This whole situation was weird, fraught. An understatement, actually.

Michael and I had a certain synergy. I thought

I understood him, or could at least predict what he might do or say. He was either resentful, displeased, or, on some very rare occasions, willing to give someone praise if they did a good enough job.

Simple.

Easy.

Except nothing about this was.

Sure, I had been nursing that stubborn crush, but never, not in a million years, had I dreamed it would be reciprocated.

Even now, after the best sex of my life, I wasn't sure that it was.

It was funny because I should have been concerned about my job and what my recklessness might cost me.

Instead, I was consumed by thoughts of him, with wondering what he might think about me.

I suspected I was one of the only people not named Murphy who was brave enough or foolish enough to tell Michael exactly what I thought.

I was also smart enough to know that my doing so bothered him.

He rarely tried to hide it, and I knew that my unwillingness to bend to his will was something Michael couldn't tolerate. So last night was probably a part of that, Michael's display of dominance, a reminder he always had the upper hand.

But I didn't think that was the entire story either.

Michael wasn't that callous. I knew his reputation and had seen personally how little he cared for politeness or other people's feelings, but my gut told me he wasn't that much of an asshole.

Which left me in a conundrum, one that I turned over and over in my head as I headed to work.

How would I approach this?

Should I pretend that nothing had happened?

That would be impossible, utterly, completely impossible in every way.

To pretend that the night before hadn't happened was beyond me.

So that wasn't an option.

But knowing what I couldn't do didn't give me any idea of what I should do.

I'd have to address this. The question was how?

I tried to imagine sitting down with Michael and having a reasonable conversation, me struggling to forget how his lips felt against my skin, his warm breath against his neck, his delicious thickness filling me.

I tightened my grip on the steering wheel, tried to refocus, consider Michael's reaction. Maybe he'd say things got out of hand. Or, God forbid, apologize.

My blood ran cold at the very thought of Michael apologizing.

Before, one of my minor life's missions had been to get Michael to admit that I was right about something, but I'd never even dreamed he'd apologize. I thought of it now, imagined listening to him being polite, appropriate.

The thought made my stomach revolt.

Asshole Michael was problematic. Polite, appropriate Michael was something I never wanted to encounter.

Plus, I couldn't forget the more practical things.

What if Michael told Patrick?

Patrick and I had a polite but distant relationship, but I had no illusions about him. He was completely by the book, and more than once had made it clear he wouldn't tolerate any bullshit or drama. I could think of little that would fit that definition more than me sleeping with Michael.

If Patrick got wind of this, I would be out on my ass, and I wasn't sure I could count on Michael to shield me. Didn't know if my pride wanted him to.

Losing my job would suck. I liked the people I worked with, liked the relative autonomy that Patrick, and even Michael gave me. I was certain I would find another job. I was very good at what I did, so unemployment wasn't a concern.

The idea of not seeing Michael was unthinkable.

Further proof I needed to get my head examined.

Michael Murphy was off-limits.

There were reasons for that. Professional ones, like the fact that his family signed my checks and I knew better than to put my financial well-being on the line for sex.

There were other reasons as well, ones I'd be stupid to not take into account.

No one spoke about the Murphys and their other "business" in the hotel. And, to the best of my knowledge, none of that stuff happened on M.'s grounds.

But a personal relationship…

That was entirely different, potentially dangerous territory.

Their lives might have looked quiet, staid from the outside, but I couldn't rely on that. Starting something with Michael would mean opening myself to that side of him…

Would I be able to?

I parked and walked into the hotel, telling myself to slow down. I was contemplating my life as a mob wife, and Michael and I had never even been on a date.

That helped temper me some, remind me I needed to take things step by step.

I'd focus on doing my job. Catch up on any emergencies that cropped up and let the rhythm of my day crowd out any thoughts of Michael.

Not thinking about him was a near impossibility, something I was reminded of when my eyes strayed toward his office unerringly. It looked like he wasn't there, and I felt some relief.

My inbox was full when I opened my computer, and I nearly cheered. I had plenty of reason not to be in my office should Michael happen to appear.

Less than five minutes after I arrived in my office, I left and made my way to the hotel kitchen, looking over my shoulder furtively, searching for any sign of Michael.

I was disappointed that I didn't see him, but soon turned my mind to work, hoping at least to find some refuge there.

The kitchen was humming with activity, as it always was.

M. Lounge and Hotel provided full service 24/7, and in the kitchen, it could be three in the morning, three in the afternoon, or anytime in between. The place was always abuzz with activity.

"Hey, Eden," Henry, the kitchen manager called when I entered.

"Good morning, Henry. What's the problem?" I asked.

He nodded and walked me through the line to the back where the kitchen equipment was.

"I have two washers down," Henry said, pointing at a huge metal box.

I followed Henry as he walked toward the box and watched as he pulled up one of the stainless-steel doors where the dishes where stacked and then washed.

He reached in, pulled out what had to be an eight-inch butcher knife.

"I found this in the motor," he said.

I looked at the knife, which was bent in the middle and looked like it would break if touched. "I could see that being problematic," I said. I didn't want to overreact, but I was alarmed. That definitely could have hurt someone, and it seemed unusual for someone on the staff to be so careless.

"Yeah. There's one over here too," Henry said.

He walked to the second machine and reached into the drawer and pulled out a similar knife.

"There was one in each of them?" I asked, some of my exasperation coming through.

"Yeah," he replied. "They're both busted. We're down to one."

"How far behind will this push you?" I asked.

"The weekend is coming up," Henry said.

He didn't need to say anything else.

Weekends were the busiest time at the hotel and there was little margin for error.

"Approve more overtime for the kitchen staff. You'll have to do this by hand until I can get replacements. Then make sure everyone is trained on how to use this equipment. That kind of thing shouldn't happen, let alone twice," I said.

"Will do. Thanks, Eden," Henry said.

I nodded, then made my way back to the executive suite, thinking about this.

Replacing equipment wouldn't be a problem, but I still felt somewhat nervous. It was my own doing. I really was confident in my ability, but this kind of stuff always made me worry. I took it personally when there were issues in the hotel, knew that poorly trained staff reflected on me. Ultimately, everything that happened here did.

Fortunately, or maybe unfortunately for me, when I got back to my office, I didn't have to worry about running into Michael.

I was so busy, that even if I had stood still long enough, I wouldn't have had a chance to talk to him.

Between people missing shifts, demanding guests, and other issues that only I could handle, I was on my feet for almost the entire day.

"Long day," Gerald said late in the afternoon.

"Yeah," I replied.

"Is everything under control?" he asked.

"Yeah, I've put out most of the fires. The new equipment is coming in, and a couple of guests need some extra attention. But everything's good," I said.

Not ten seconds later, the phone rang.

I groaned, looked at the receiver but then picked it up.

"What now?" I asked.

I could hear Shelly, the switchboard operator's smile through the phone.

"There's a water pressure issue on the tenth floor," she said.

"Did you call maintenance?" I asked.

"I did. The guys are out to lunch," she replied.

I frowned but kept my voice calm. "Thanks for letting me know, Shelly. I'll take care of it," I said.

I hung up the phone, stood.

Gerald looked at me, concerned. "Is everything okay?"

"It's fine," I said, giving him a smile that I didn't quite feel.

As I headed down to the basement, I remembered my mother's admonition about being careful what I wished for.

"You were right about that, Mama," I whispered.

FIFTEEN

MICHAEL

I'd searched everywhere for Eden, who was nowhere to be found. It was late, so it was reasonable to think she'd gone home, but she hadn't. I wasn't sure how I knew that, but I did. So I'd set off twenty minutes ago, eager to ask her some question that I'd already forgotten.

When I hadn't found her immediately, I hadn't been able to let it go, and now, as I roamed the halls, whatever it was that had made me seek her out was no longer important.

I just needed to see her.

I told myself that it was nothing, simply a manifestation of my hatred of being denied anything, but for the first time, I wasn't sure that I believed it.

So, instead of thinking about that, about what it might mean, I continued to search for her, becoming increasingly irritated with each moment that passed.

I'd looked on all the floors, in the office area, then the kitchen. I nodded at several hotel employees, but hadn't asked any of them about her whereabouts. I didn't want to appear anxious, and asking about her would have felt like a defeat.

I wouldn't let Eden defeat me. Wouldn't let anyone defeat me.

Of course, that determination to not give even the hint of an upper hand was working against me now because Eden was still nowhere in sight.

I paused in the hallway, my heart beating far too fast. I could feel the way my features twisted with my angst, felt like the fucking tie Patrick insisted I wear was choking me.

I stomped back to my office and ripped of the tie and jacket and popped the first two buttons on my shirt, thankful to at least not have that constricting me anymore.

Then, I set off in search of Eden again, even angrier now.

What the hell was wrong with her? Didn't she know she might be needed? Leaving like that with no one knowing where she was, that was fucking stupid and even more frustrating.

I prepared to search the floors again, thinking I'd missed her. When I stopped at the stairs that led to the basement, I came up short.

The basement was off-limits to guests and employees that weren't specifically authorized to go down there.

Eden was authorized.

I literally saw red as I pushed the heavy door open and ran down the stairs, each step sending my anger past the boiling point.

She'd better not be down there. She had no reason to be and it was far too dangerous for her to be down there alone.

When I reached the bottom of the stairs, I followed a sound that I instinctively knew was her. The impulse to run was strong, but I forced myself to slow my steps, both to buy me time to calm down and to make sure I didn't seem too excited.

Because as pissed as I was, and I was fucking pissed, I wanted to see her, but didn't know if I could handle her knowing that.

After what felt like an eternity, I rounded the corner and stopped when I saw Eden.

Her hair was still pulled back in that prim and

proper bun, the little pearl earrings spotting her delicate lobes.

But she'd taken off her ever-present blazer and button-down shirt, and wore only a thin, almost sheer shirt that gave a perfect view of her full breasts lovingly held by her lace bra, along with the sweep of brown skin that was glistening with sweat.

In an instant, I was rock-hard, the instant desire for her, the anger that hadn't lessened a bit, a dizzying combination.

"What the fuck are you doing?"

Eden let out a little shriek that would have been adorable had I not been so pissed. She dropped her hands and then turned to face me, her tits jiggling enticingly when she did.

"Jesus, Michael. You scared me—"

"I asked you a question, Eden. What are you doing?" I barked.

She stiffened, her eyes widening. Then, she seemed to recover and pointed at a valve attached to the wall.

"I was trying to turn this. A guest on the tenth floor is having an issue, and I wanted to—"

"Are you a fucking plumber?"

She frowned, looked taken aback by my tone, but I didn't care.

"No, but—"

"I have staff for this, Eden. Do you know how fucking stupid it is for you to be down here by yourself?"

She ignored my question and said, "It's an easy fix, and the maintenance staff is at dinner. I just thought—"

"You weren't thinking," I snapped, pissed that she was so thoughtless, didn't seem to have a care about her safety.

Eden looked wounded, something that gave me a moment's pause, but only a moment's. It wasn't safe for her to be down here alone, and besides, this wasn't her job.

Still, the stunned look in her eyes touched me, made me want to soothe it away. I couldn't do that, wouldn't let myself, so I did the next best thing.

"What's the problem?" I asked, walking until I stood in front of the valve.

"This should be a half degree warmer," she said quietly. "I just need to turn it one notch. That should do it."

I wasn't surprised that Eden knew exactly what the problem was, or that she'd felt compelled to try to fix it herself. I might even have been a little impressed, but she'd still been stupid to come down here by herself.

She reached up, but I lifted my hand and shook my head, making sure not to look at her. Then, I turned the valve.

"You happy now?" I asked when I finally looked at her, choosing to focus on my own irritation at her stubborn independence and not the fact that I was again alone with her.

"I…" she trailed off, hesitated. "I…"

She looked up at me with dark eyes, and I did the only thing I could.

In one motion, I locked my hand behind her head and covered her lips with mine.

———

EDEN

One moment, Michael was staring at me so intently, I thought he might throttle me.

The next, he was kissing me, the kiss as angry as his eyes had been.

That should have been enough to make me push him away.

It wasn't.

I didn't know what to make of Michael's reaction, had no idea what he was even reacting to, but in that moment, I didn't care. Couldn't care, couldn't do anything but take his kiss, his lips bruising, almost punishing against mine, his hand rough against my breast. And like always, I responded to his wild roughness. Would have reached out to touch him, but couldn't because he'd trapped both of my hands in one of his. His strength thrilled me, as did the wonder of what he planned to do next.

But, just as suddenly as the kiss had begun, it ended.

Michael broke away and stared down at me, his night-sky eyes as stormy as I'd ever seen them, his chest heaving. It was warm in the basement, but I didn't think the heat was the reason for the flush that brightened his face.

Maybe it was anger, but as many times as Michael had looked at me in anger, it had never looked like this. His expression now was tumultuous, angry, yet not. Something in me wanted to reach out to him, soothe that tumult, so I tried to pull my hand free, planned to brush the lock of dark hair that lay against his forehead away. Hoped that maybe that touch would be calming to him.

I didn't have the chance.

When I tried to reach up, he tightened his grip,

and then in the next breath, I was facing the wall, Michael's huge body caging me between it and him.

"Michael—"

My words died in my throat when he jammed his hand between my thighs and cupped my pussy.

I was dripping for him, needy for the feeling that only he could bring. I didn't understand it, didn't understand him, really, but this feeling, the one that only he could stir was unmistakable. Even if it was beyond the capacity of my rational mind to understand, my body did.

As if to prove the point, my hips began to roll, moving against his hand, wanting more of the delicious friction. Michael still had his hand wrapped around mine, limiting my movements, but I was too uncoordinated, probably would have been unable to do anything had I been able to move.

"That was stupid, Eden," Michael growled, his deep, raspy voice filling my ears.

My pussy clenched at the sound, and the last mindful part of me wondered how I could respond when he was taking me to task for no reason, doing something he had no right to do.

"Michael, you're being ridiculous," I said, my words breathy, not sounding at all like me.

"I'm being ridiculous?" he said, his breath warm against my ear.

"Yes," I said, pleased that I was able to speak, "you—"

Whatever I'd intended to say was lost when he twisted my clit, soothed away the sting with his fingers. And when he kissed my neck, his lips so soft, such a great contrast to the roughness of his fingers and his voice, my knees buckled.

I barely moved though, Michael's strong grip on my wrists holding me in place.

I was flat against the wall, my breasts smashed against the concrete, the press relieving some of the ache that made my nipples throb. I was so distracted by the feeling of his heavy hand against my nipple, it took a moment for me to realize he'd turned me.

"That was idiotic, even," Michael whispered, his breath warm against my skin as he nuzzled my breasts and kissed down my satin camisole.

"Are you… Are you lecturing me right now?" I asked, my breath coming out on a hitch.

Still, I was surprised I had managed to speak, what with the way he was driving me to distraction.

"Yes, I am. That was stupid. Don't do anything like that again," he said.

He sounded easy-breezy, nothing of his voice betraying the fact he had hooked his hands into my waistband and was pulling my panties down my hips as he spoke.

"Michael. You're being ridic—" I cut off on a nod as he kneeled and pressed his lips between my thighs.

He dove in, kissed my slit, my inner thighs.

"You were saying?" he asked a moment later when he pulled back and looked up at me, his lips glistening from my wetness.

"I…"

I trailed off, swallowed thickly, bit my lip when he smirked.

"As I thought," he whispered, his breath tickling the hair that covered my sex.

I shivered, a sensation that intensified when he did so again and then pressed his lips against my sex.

Michael kissed me slowly, almost reverently, the gentle caress, smooth glide of his lips against my pussy so different than the insistent tap of his finger against my clit.

I reached out, my hands landing on his shoulders as I looked at him, desperate for something to hold onto.

"Michael..." I said.

He huffed out a chuckle but I didn't pay attention, couldn't care, not when he was doing this to me. Michael worked me over slowly, lapped at every inch of my pussy until I was a keening, wailing mess.

When he squeezed my clit between his fingers, I went off like a rocket, exploding in a climax that left me breathless. Michael kissed me, petted me as I rode my climax down.

After one last kiss against my quivering sex, he stood, stared at me for a long moment before he leaned forward and kissed me deeply, possessively. Kissed me until I was breathless, clinging to him, desperate for more.

He broke away, trailing his lips against my ear.

"You want me to fuck you right here don't you?" he whispered.

"Yes," I responded without hesitation, my breath coming out heavy.

He met my eyes. "Maybe if you're not so stupid next time."

I glared at him, glared harder when he smirked.

"Asshole," I muttered, my face beginning to flame as Michael looked at me knowingly.

He just smirked harder, then pulled my panties up and slid my skirt down.

"Let's go," he said.

SIXTEEN

MICHAEL

A FEW DAYS LATER, well into the evening, I was preparing to leave the hotel.

I'd seen Eden twice in those days, and only fleeting glimpses. I couldn't shake the feeling she was trying to avoid me. Or maybe I was just using that as an excuse to avoid her. Either way, I kept my distance, not exactly hiding from her but not seeking her out either.

It had been a struggle, the need to see her, hear her voice, touch her again, testing me. And now, my patience had been exhausted. She'd probably be gone by now, but that didn't keep me from looking for her or feeling a moment's triumph when I found her car in the parking lot.

The truth was, I was slowly losing my mind.

That taste of Eden, those precious, treasured moments hadn't been nearly enough.

Worse, so much worse that I didn't want to even admit it to myself, I missed her. Eden drove me crazy, seemed to make it her mission to do so. But those few days of silence, of not having her there were nearly unbearable, and were something I wasn't anxious to continue.

I entered her office, found Gerald sitting at their shared desk. There was no sign of Eden.

"Where is she?" I asked.

Gerald had heard my approach even though he pretended otherwise. He looked up, gave me the falsest fucking smile I'd ever seen. Annoying, but I didn't care because Gerald was going to tell me where Eden was.

"Good evening, Mr. Murphy. I'd have thought you would be handling…other affairs at this hour," he said.

"Where is she?" I repeated, letting some of my annoyance bleed into my voice.

I needed to see Eden and I wouldn't let this prick slow me down.

"I believe she's gone for the evening," he finally said.

Bullshit, but I didn't know if Gerald was screwing with me or if he was just oblivious. It might have been both.

Eden covered for him, but I knew she was the one who did the bulk of the work. He probably didn't know where she was, and even if he did, I doubted he would tell me. He hated my guts, though I didn't care. Patrick had kept him for continuity, and I didn't force the issue because I knew how much she cared for him.

Gerald knew that, which meant he also probably knew that Eden or not, one step too far and I'd toss him out on his ass.

I said nothing else and left, deciding I would find Eden myself.

I checked the basement first, knowing I wouldn't find her there, a little disappointed when I didn't. She had no business down there by herself, but if she had been, it would have been the perfect excuse to bend her over my desk and spank that deliciously round ass.

Of course, I didn't need a reason, decided I would do just that as soon as I found her.

If I found her.

Fifteen minutes later, I was increasingly agitated that Eden seemed to be nowhere. I checked the employee lounge, the kitchen, and the security room.

No Eden.

So I went to housekeeping, the only other place she could possibly be.

When I rounded the corner into the large room stacked high with shelves on a concrete floor, my heart thudded, the relief at seeing her only serving to remind me how much I had needed to.

Her hair was pulled back like always, her jacket buttoned tight, everything about her crisp, professional, even as she struggled with what looked like a hundred pounds of linen.

I moved to her quickly, grabbed it from her hands.

"What are you doing, Eden?" I said, remembering to leave the curse out, though it hovered on the tip of my tongue.

"Hello, Michael. I'm loading this cart," she said, like the answer was obvious.

I frowned. "That shit's way too heavy for you to lift."

"No it's not. I've done it many times before,"

she said, reaching for the stack that I had lifted away from her.

She frowned in response, looking impatient, and, I noticed, exhausted. "It's a part of the job."

"Not yours," I replied.

"Well that's where you and I disagree, Mr. Murphy," she said haughtily. "As assistant general manager, my job is to make sure that everything runs smoothly, and sometimes that means loading carts or cleaning rooms. Doing whatever it takes."

Hearing her say that reminded me of those years ago when she'd said pretty much the same thing to Patrick. I'd barely paid attention, but even then, I'd been certain he would keep her. In all of our businesses, Patrick appreciated someone who was willing to do what it took to see that the job was done. That was definitely Eden.

Even to her own detriment, apparently. As I looked at her more, I could see that I'd been right. She still had her professional veneer, but her eyes weren't quite as lively as usual, her posture not as straight.

"What were you about to do?" I asked.

"Finish loading this cart and then deliver it to the eighth floor. There's a broken one up there and I want to replace it," she said.

"I'll do it," I said, speaking the words before I had really considered them, but knowing they were right. I could press the point that this wasn't her job, but she'd feel compelled to argue the point, and as fun as arguing with Eden could be, I'd rather get this done so Eden would rest.

She looked at me, surprised. "That's not necessary, Michael," she finally said.

"It is. Eden, you look—"

She shook her head to cut me off, stood up straighter, stiffly.

"Michael, I don't need your opinion of how I look," she said.

That feeling that I had seen in her face before was back, and that question that I had before was there.

"You always say it's rude to interrupt," I said, tossing back words she'd thrown at me a hundred times before, shocked that I'd ever had occasion to use them.

She smiled, her expression sheepish, though I could still see her exhaustion. "Touché," she said, conceding the point with a grace I could never hope to match.

"What did you think I was going to say?" I

asked, suspecting I knew the answer but wanting to hear her say it.

Her smile dampened. "It's not important."

"It's important because I asked. So answer," I said.

She looked at me furtively, not even mentioning my tone, then looked down. She breathed deep, which only made me that much more anxious to know what she had thought. After a moment, she looked up at me again.

"I guess I just supposed you're going to point out some flaw with my appearance," she said.

She powered through the words, managing to speak almost nonchalantly, though I could see the toll they took on her. I didn't like the idea of them hurting her at all.

"Eden, you're not that stupid, are you?" I said.

She frowned. "I'd like to think I'm not stupid at all, but it seems you differ."

"That depends," I responded, knowing it was probably my fault that she thought that but disappointed she didn't know better.

"On?" she asked, her eyes bright now, some of the exhaustion receding as she tried to figure out whether to be pissed at me or not.

"On how good you are at picking up on cues," I said.

She quirked her brow, her question clear.

"Eden, if there was ever a question, it should be obvious by now I don't find any fault with your appearance," I said.

"You don't?" she whispered, before she jumped, seeming surprised she had said the words out loud.

"No, I don't," I responded, but only after I had given her a slow, thorough, head-to-toe appraisal before meeting her eyes again.

"Then what? And before, when you asked why I looked like that? What did that mean?"

I smiled, finding that I enjoyed having the upper hand on Eden even as I hated having given her any reason to doubt herself, even if only by accident.

"If you would have bothered to listen, you would have known I thought you looked tired. Too tired," I said quietly.

"Really?" she asked, her skepticism clear.

"Really," I responded.

She wrinkled her brows, looked at me in a way I couldn't quite understand or describe.

"I am. Things have been a little hectic," she said tentatively.

"Then ask for help," I said sharply, knowing she was too stubborn to do so but intent on making sure she knew how idiotic that was.

She stiffened, her eyes wide, and I lowered my voice. "It's good that you're dedicated, but you shouldn't try to do everybody's job, Eden. If you need something just ask for it," I said.

"You'll listen?" she asked.

"What do you think?"

She looked at me riotously, and then smiled. "Honestly...?"

"No, lie to me," I said.

She pushed my arm playfully, the action friendly, one that spoke of an ease between us that I found I quite welcomed.

"Whatever," she said. Then she sobered. "We need some more housekeepers. And another maintenance man. People like the extra hours, but we're running thin."

"Why didn't you say something sooner?" I asked.

"I wasn't in the mood to fight, and didn't have the time for it anyway," she said.

I went quiet then, thought about that answer, how much I didn't like it. Thought about all the things I wanted to say to her, things I knew I never would.

"Go home, Eden," I said instead.

"I will," she replied, nodding. "Just as soon as—"

"Now," I said, using my most stern voice.

She looked at me for a moment, then another, and then finally nodded. "If you insist, Mr. Murphy."

SEVENTEEN

EDEN

Michael had sent me home to rest, but I had done anything but.

All night I had tossed and turned, my mind spinning, my body on fire with thoughts of him.

Seeing him had been a surprise. If I was honest, I could acknowledge that I'd been hiding from him, something I'd thought was justified. I hadn't known how he would react, didn't know how I would, so I'd thought it best to stay away.

But staying away had done nothing to banish thoughts of Michael. I'd replayed those moments in the boiler room, both the hotel and the actual pub, over and over again. Had thought of little else.

I had no idea what was happening between us, couldn't say for sure that anything was happening between us and didn't have the nerve to seek him out.

But then, last night, when Michael, in his own particular way, had expressed something like care toward me, it changed me. I hadn't seen that side of him, and I found that I appreciated it, liked it.

Liked him.

Even after what we had shared, it was nearly impossible to imagine, but it occurred to me that maybe, just possibly, Michael was more than the cantankerous, annoying jerk he pretended to be.

Oh, he was all those things, but he was more, and I'd gotten glimpses of that, glimpses that pulled me in even more.

As I dressed the next morning, I told myself I needed to stop this. Needed to keep my wits about me.

Michael might have different sides, but those didn't erase the years of experience I had with him, and it would be foolish of me to pretend they did.

It would be hard, nearly impossible, especially given how much I wanted him, but I would keep my distance, make sure that I didn't fall into his bed again, at least not until I had a better idea of what I was dealing with.

I wasn't foreclosing anything with Michael, but

I couldn't let myself get sucked in by emotion, wouldn't allow my body to overrule my mind. That admonishment firmly in mind, I drove to work, happy, confident in the decision I had made.

Most mornings, I parked in the very back of the employee lot, an area that was usually deserted. Today, though, I noticed several trucks around the loading dock. I watched them curiously, nodded at the deliverymen as I walked inside.

The replacement kitchen equipment had arrived the day before, and I hadn't scheduled anything for today. Perhaps Gerald would have an idea of what was going on.

I went inside quickly and found Gerald in our office. He stood in the center of the room, something I might have found odd if I wasn't used to it by now. He was dressed crisply as usual, but his expression practically screamed his displeasure.

"Is everything okay, Gerald? Did you have a delivery scheduled for today?" I asked.

"I did not," he replied stiffly. "It seems that was Mr. Murphy's doing."

"Really? Did he say what it was?" I asked, wondering what it could be.

Gerald's already frowning face dropped farther, his disgust palpable. "It seems Mr. Murphy finds some of our equipment unsuitable. He said the housekeeping carts were, and I quote, 'shit.' He ordered replacements for all of them."

"He did!" I exclaimed, excitement starting to brew.

"Yes. Can you believe that?" he replied, almost sputtering with anger.

"I can't, but the staff is going to be so excited! Those other carts really were unwieldy," I said.

Gerald looked wounded, and I moved in to soothe his feelings, belatedly remembering that Gerald had handpicked those carts long before I had come to the hotel. I plastered on a smile. "The others were perfectly fine, but there are newer, more modern ones that will be easier for the staff to maneuver, and if they can move quickly, that leaves more space to give our guests the best possible experience," I said, going back to the thing Gerald preached above all others.

That seemed to placate him some, which was the best that I could do. I had told him we needed new carts for a couple of years now, but he'd always insisted the expense was unnecessary. I was glad to have them, but even more, I was excited Michael had acted so decisively about something that would be so beneficial for the staff.

"And that's not all," Gerald said, his voice heading off the dreamy thoughts I was about to fall into. That was a good thing. What Michael had done was considerate, but it didn't qualify him for sainthood or even make him a good guy, so I needed to keep some perspective.

When I looked at Gerald again, he wore an expression of shock and horror so extreme, it threatened laughter.

"There," he said, nodding toward the closed door of the suite across the hall.

"What?" I asked, following his gaze.

"According to him, you informed him we need additional housekeepers and a maintenance man, so he's sent over applicants," Gerald said, sniffing over the word "applicants."

I was far too excited to pay him any attention, though.

The carts were one thing. I took Michael at his word when he'd said he was going to deliver it, so that meant he'd had firsthand experience trying to move those things.

But sending over new staff... That was something I had mentioned offhand when I was borderline exhausted, and less than twelve hours later, he'd made it happen.

If he'd done all this for me, it would have been the most romantic gesture anyone had ever done for me. But I couldn't allow myself to think it. Michael's interest was his hotel and seeing that it was the best it could possibly be. It had nothing to do with me, and I would not, could not, let myself forget that.

"Would you like to sit in on interviews?" I asked Gerald.

He shook his head. "No, that won't be necessary. I'm sure you'll take care of it. I'll go do the rounds."

"Okay. But this is good, Gerald. Remember how we used to talk about how we'd manage things if we had the resources?" I said, recalling some of Gerald's and my conversations about that topic.

He nodded stiffly, grudgingly, but I overlooked that and smiled.

"This is our chance," I said, reaching out to touch his arm but stopping myself before I did, not sure of how Gerald would respond.

He didn't at first, but then pressed his lips into a thin line. "You're right as always, Eden," he said. "I'll get to those rounds now."

I watched him as he left, certain that there was more to Gerald's reaction.

I'd have to talk to him, see what was going on. I knew that change was tough for Gerald, but this was a good thing. Yes, Michael was overbearing, but it seemed he had the staff's best interest at heart, and as soon as I got Gerald to accept that, I knew he'd be happy about the state of the hotel.

Until then, I had new staff to interview. Then I needed to find Michael.

———

EDEN

Four hours and five new employees later, I ventured out of the executive suite, headed directly for Michael's office, my excitement propelling me.

I didn't even slow down long enough to get lunch.

I'd do that later, but the need to see Michael even outweighed hunger.

When I reached his door, I stood still, the nerves I almost always had when I knew I was going to see him present, but this time was different. I was excited, anxious to see him.

"Get a grip, Eden," I mumbled to myself.

A fraction of a second later, the door swung

open, and I looked up in surprise to meet Michael's eyes.

"Are you outside of my door talking to yourself, Eden?" he asked.

"I—um—I…" I looked at him, smiled. "Guilty as charged," I said.

"Come in," he said, turning to walk to his desk.

His broad shoulders filled out his suit jacket and I remembered what it was like to wrap my arms around them, hold them as he pushed himself inside me.

Then tried to remind myself that this was not the time or the place to think such things.

"Eden!" Michael snapped impatiently.

"What? I'm sorry," I said, focusing on Michael who had turned and stood staring at me.

"You haven't had lunch. Should I order you something?" he said.

"No, that won't be nec—"

The grumble of my stomach cut me off, and Michael gave me a knowing smirk and then picked up the phone.

"Add an additional plate to my lunch order," he said. Then he hung up the phone.

"You didn't say thank you," I said.

"No, I didn't. Is that your way of distracting me?" he asked, his expression almost a smile.

It had been, and to my surprise, Michael hadn't gone for it.

"Maybe," I said, smiling at him.

"Yeah. Nice try," he said. "You shouldn't go so long without eating. You've been in the conference room since you arrived."

"Keeping tabs on me, Mr. Murphy?" I asked.

"You're in my hotel. Of course I am," he said.

There had been a time when him saying something like that would have set me off, but this time I smiled, feeling cared for in a way I seldom did, and walked to sit at the conference table where Michael had taken a seat.

"Thank you," I said.

"For what?" he asked.

"For the new equipment, the new staff," I responded.

"It's my hotel. The staff and the equipment are going to make it run better. So why would you thank me for that?" he asked, his expression one that seemed to suggest he thought I was being ridiculous. It was one I was quite familiar with.

"I don't know. Maybe because it's the polite thing to do," I said, my voice sounding peevish.

When Michael smiled, I thought I would sink into the floor. "I took the bait didn't I?"

"Hook, line, and sinker," he said.

Then he laughed, the expression so different, so welcome.

We went quiet for a moment, the silence almost but not quite awkward.

There shouldn't have been anything awkward about it.

After the things this man had done to me, something as commonplace as a joke shouldn't have left me flustered. But it did.

Michael did.

That in and of itself wasn't unusual, and in fact was something I should have expected. If nothing else, Michael had always been able to keep me on my toes. But there was something about this, a new level of intimacy that had never been there before, one I was still trying to feel my way through.

"Come in," Michael called when a soft knock on the door broke the silence.

"I have your lunch, Mr. Murphy," Henry, the kitchen manager said. Then he looked at me and nodded. "Eden."

"Hey, Henry," I replied, feeling even more awkward now.

Henry's expression hadn't told me anything, but I knew that meant nothing. In our line of work, we ran into pretty much anything and not allowing a response to show was a tool of the trade.

But maybe Henry wasn't reacting because there was nothing to react to. Michael and I met all the time.

This was no different.

I told myself that but knew it was an utter lie.

This was different, and as Henry deposited the plates on the conference table, it occurred to me why.

This wasn't owner and assistant general manager having a meeting over lunch. It wasn't even some-times-adversaries taking a break from hostilities for a meal.

This was a date.

If Henry hadn't been in the room, I might have cursed.

At no point had I contemplated a date with Michael being on the afternoon agenda, and I hadn't slept nearly enough to be ready for it.

I glanced at Michael, who looked back at me, his expression stony.

Whether I had contemplated it or not, here it

was, and it didn't look like Michael had any interest in throwing me a lifeline.

"I'll drop by later this afternoon, see how that new equipment is working out," I said as Henry left.

It was a pathetic and wholly ineffective attempt to make this something other than what it clearly was.

"Sure thing," he replied and then he was gone.

When he left, I was in the bizarre position of being both relieved and more nervous.

"You don't want people getting the wrong idea, huh?" Michael said.

"What makes you think that?" I replied, managing to hold his gaze through a feat of sheer will.

Michael smirked. "Eden, you're a terrible bull-shitter. Your face tells everything you're thinking. You're worried old Henry there will figure out that you're banging me," he said.

The slight crudeness of his words was a complete contrast with the way he folded the napkin across his legs, but then, what was Michael if not a study in contrasts?

"First off, I'm not 'banging' you," I said.

"You're technically correct. You aren't at this exact moment," he said.

The tenor of his voice gave me hope that that might soon change, hope that I, with a great deal of effort, ignored.

"You think pretty highly of yourself, don't you, Mr. Murphy?" I said, mimicking his motion with the napkin, though I couldn't quite pull it off.

Then I watched, mesmerized as he sliced a Brussels sprout in half with practiced, precise movements.

"Did they teach you that at boarding school or something?" I asked.

"Teach me what?" Michael responded.

He looked at me after he'd taken a bite of the vegetable, reminding me I'd spoken with my mouth full and that I hadn't even bothered to slice my own.

The irony was not lost on me. I'd had an image of Michael, a crude man in a nice suit, and here he was, giving me a silent lesson on table manners.

I smiled, then shrugged, deciding to let it drop. "Nothing. I was just saying you probably went to a fancy school or something," I said.

Michael laughed heartily and then ate another

Brussels sprout. "A boarding school? One that taught table manners?"

"Yeah," I said.

"Right. Probably paid for with old money, right? Only the best of the best for the Murphys?"

I shrugged. "Well..."

"Well what?" he asked, his amusement clear.

"I mean, you own a hotel. I think Sean owns that pub. You're not hurting or anything. Forget I said anything," I said, hating how presumptuous I sounded.

"I own a hotel now, but the closest I or any of my brothers have ever gotten to boarding school is juvenile detention," he said.

It wasn't surprising, especially given all the rumors, but that didn't fit with what I saw of him.

"You don't buy it?" he said.

"I mean...you put your napkin across your lap," I said, feeling so unbelievably lame. Michael just laughed, his response putting me at ease. "You can thank Patrick for that," he said.

"How so?" I asked.

"He looks tough but he's Miss fuckin' Manners. He made us learn all that crap," Michael said.

"Really?" I asked, furrowing my brows as I tried

to process this new piece of information, one that gave me welcome insight into Michael.

"Yeah, he said it might come in handy one day. That we couldn't just rely on—" He cut off before he finished and shoved the last of his Brussels sprouts into his mouth.

I was burning with curiosity about what he'd been about to say, but I didn't want to push him, ruin this moment too soon. Instead I looked at his plate.

"You ate all your vegetables first," I said.

He laughed again, the tension that had looked to be on the verge of taking hold receding.

"Old habit," he said.

I lifted a brow in question.

"Another thing to thank Patrick for. He also insisted that we get proper nutrition, which meant eating vegetables. For a while, I just made Sean eat mine, but then Patrick caught on. He'd watch to make sure I ate them, so I just forced them down to get them out of the way," he said.

I laughed, trying to imagine a younger, probably brooding Michael eating his broccoli at his older brother's behest.

"So Patrick took care of you?" I asked.

"Yeah," he said.

He went quiet then, and though I was still burning with questions, I didn't ask more.

"What about you?" Michael said a moment later.

"What about me?" I responded.

"Who taught you how to lay your napkin across your lap?"

I laughed, looked at him.

"No one. My mother was a free spirit. She didn't care about that kind of stuff," I said.

"How did you end up here?" he asked.

"Happenstance, really. I always loved hotels when I was a kid, though the ones we stayed in were nothing like M.," I said.

"You moved from place to place?" he asked.

"Yeah. Like I said, my mother was a free spirit," I replied.

Michael's expression darkened and I shook my head quickly. "It's nothing like that. She was a wonderful mother and lived life to the fullest. She told me the world was too big to be planted in one place, so we went on a bunch of adventures."

"What happened?" The tone of Michael's voice told me that he heard the wistfulness I still felt when I thought of her.

"She passed away when I was twenty. I loved

our life, but I wanted to put down roots, and I found a place to do that in this hotel," I said.

"That's why you stuck around for so long when this place was in the shitter, right?"

"I don't know if I'd say it was in the shitter, but that's semantics. Yeah, I loved this place, and even when it was more budget friendly, it was nice to give people a good experience even if they couldn't afford top dollar," I said.

"Huh," he said, his expression telling me he was pondering something. "We should give away some suites sometimes."

I brightened, excited at the prospect. "That would be awesome! Most people can't really afford this place, so it would be a nice treat," I said.

"I'll talk to Patrick about it," Michael responded.

His eyes darkened, and he pushed his plate aside, then neatly folded his napkin, laid it on the conference table.

"Eden—"

The tinny static from my walkie-talkie cut him off.

"Eden, where are you?" Gerald said, his voice like a bucket of ice water.

Or in Michael's case, logs on the fire.

I stood and fumbled in my pocket, looking for the walkie-talkie.

Michael stood too and walked the few feet that separated us.

"This fucking guy…" he mumbled as he pulled the walkie-talkie from my pocket.

"Wait!" I said. "I need to—"

I cut off and started laughing as Michael turned the walkie-talkie off and took out the battery for good measure.

When he looked at me, he shook his head. "I should fire that asshole. Making you laugh was not what I had in mind," he said.

I locked eyes with him, my laughter gone, need, uncertainty, taking its place.

"What did you have in mind?" I asked.

Michael lifted one corner of his mouth, walked closer. Stopped when there was less than an inch between us. "You must have some idea," he whispered, his face impassive but his voice practically caressing me.

I met his eyes. Gave him a smile of my own, one that I hoped showed how much I wanted him, *needed* him in this moment.

"I do," I said.

"So what did you have in mind?" Michael

asked. His usually serious exterior had given way to playfulness, playfulness that I also felt.

"Oh, I don't know, Mr. Murphy," I said, lifting my hand to cup his hardness. "Let me surprise you," I said.

"I don't like surprises, Eden," he responded.

I smiled, doing my best impersonation of the cocky expression he now wore.

"You might like this one," I said, my stomach fluttering, my sex starting to clench.

I leaned forward, pressed my lips against his neck, feeling his heartbeat under my lips, smiling when he hardened against my hand.

"Maybe," he said grudgingly.

I chuckled, kissed his neck again, feeling so very naughty in the best possible way. I wasn't the kind of woman to do things like this, but when I was with Michael, I felt different, free to be wanton.

It didn't matter that I was wearing my serviceable loafers and work uniform. That I was still the same old Eden I'd always been. When I touched Michael like this, when he looked at me like he was now, I felt precious, treasured.

Now, I wanted to make him feel what I did. Or at least try to.

I boldly squeezed his cock with my hand.

He looked at me, lifted a brow, and then nodded slightly. I could see that he was allowing me to set the tone.

And so I would.

I moved my hands up, and unbuckled his pants, moving slow, calmly, like I was in complete control, though I was nervous, so turned on, I was jittery, wanting Michael with an intensity that took my breath away.

It was funny because we both knew where this was headed, but I didn't want to give him the advantage, as I knew he wouldn't want to give it to me. So we would continue on in this little battle, and I was determined to win this round.

I unfastened his pants, lowered them and his underwear enough to reveal his stiff shaft.

I reached for him boldly, sighing at his warm, heavy weight in my palm.

When I heard his sharp intake of breath, I looked up to meet his eyes.

He kept his expression disinterested, which was impressive, given how his cock throbbed in my hand, precum leaking from his tip profusely.

Though he was keeping his cool, I could see that I was pushing him, see that he was on the edge.

He growled when I released him, but then

smiled when, without pause I lowered myself to my knees.

When I looked up at him, I saw that this position pleased him.

I liked it too, something that surprised me. So much of Michael's and my relationship was a battle, but being like this in front of him, yet still in control, was powerfully arousing, made me feel treasured.

But instead of examining the feelings Michael so easily managed to stir, I braced myself, putting one hand on either of his thighs.

Then I leaned forward, breathed deep, taking in his masculine scent. I nudged the tip of his cock with my lips, then placed gentle kisses against his cockhead, then down, brushing my lips against his shaft.

"Eden," Michael said, his voice thick, grumbling.

Gruff as always, but I was firmly in control, something I reminded him of when I didn't increase my pace.

Instead I kept my motions leisurely, softly kissing his shaft, moving up, then down, teasing him from root to shaft and back up again.

I moved even slower when he thrust his hips up,

his demand clear. I laughed softly, feeling more powerful, more beautiful and desired than I ever had before. It seemed almost unfathomable that I was in this position, that Michael wanted me and that I was enjoying this so much.

But I was and I would continue to.

"Eden," Michael said again, thrusting his hips again, sending his cock against my lips.

I looked into his eyes, saw the burning fire there and decided to take mercy on him. I opened my mouth and took him inside.

His thickness and length filled my mouth, but I took as much of him as I could, worked him as deep as I could without gagging. I sealed my lips and worked my jaw hard, swirling my tongue against his shaft. He throbbed in my mouth and I sucked harder, moaning at the taste and feel of him.

"Eden, I'm gonna come," he said, his voice thick, tense as he tried to pull away.

I clamped around him tighter, the insistent throb of his cock in my mouth telling me how close to the edge he was. I wanted to push him over, so I took him as deep as I could and tightened my hands around the base of his cock and began pumping him.

"Eden!" he said, breathing out hard as he spilled his seed down my throat.

I continued to tease him with my tongue until he softened and pulled his cock from my mouth. Then, in a smooth motion, he pulled me to my feet and kissed me until I was breathless.

EIGHTEEN

EDEN

"If that phone rings again, I'm going to scream," I said, a few weeks later, collapsing in my chair in exhaustion.

Gerald chuckled and when I looked at him, he gave me a commiserating smile.

"When it rains, it pours," he said, looking almost as weary as I felt.

"Understatement of the week," I replied as I kicked off my loafers, relieved to be out of the shoes.

They were comfortable but they weren't designed for a fourteen-hour day spent entirely on my feet, especially not the fourth one in a row.

"What is going on, Gerald?" I said.

He'd unbuttoned the top two buttons of his

shirt, proof that he really was as weary as I was. These last few days had been chaotic, with both Gerald and me rushing from one mini-disaster to the next, despite the help and equipment. We hadn't had a quiet moment. I hadn't even seen Michael in several days.

"Things have been rather active," he said. Then he smiled. "But it reminds me of the old times. The good ones."

I returned the smile. "You mean when it was just you and me and one housekeeper serving a forty-five-room hotel?" I asked.

"Indeed," he said. "I've never worked so hard in my life, but we were a good team. And we ran a good hotel."

"We still are, and we still do," I replied.

Gerald nodded, but his smile had dampened.

I studied him, and though I was exhausted, now felt like the right time to talk to him, see if I could make him feel better.

"Gerald, what's going on?" I asked.

He looked at me, his expression curious, like he was confused as to what I was asking.

"It's been a rather busy couple of days," he said.

I tilted my head, smiled at him patiently but unwilling to let him get away with such an evasive answer. "Gerald, I've known you for more than a decade."

He smiled, although sheepishly, an interesting expression for the nearly sixty-year-old man.

"Things are so different," he finally said with a sigh.

"They are," I replied, not saying anything else, deciding to let him talk.

"It's just…" He started, stopped, started again. "I know it's been a long time but it's a lot to adjust to," he said.

"I know, but we talked about this too, you know?" I responded.

"I know. But when we talked about plans, resources, how we would manage things if we had the chance to do so, I always imagined it would be us," he said.

I looked at Gerald, nodded, suddenly understanding. "And now it's not."

"No. We find ourselves with several owners. Some better than others," he said.

"Gerald, I know this isn't ideal, but the Murphys—Michael—have our best interests at heart," I said.

He studied me, his eyes unreadable. "You really believe that?" he asked.

I nodded emphatically. "I do. Think about how different things are, how much they've changed."

"I do. I do think about it," he said.

"But not just the bad stuff, or stuff you don't like, Gerald. We both make more now than we ever would have before. So does the rest of the staff. We get written up in travel magazines, and people rave about staying at our hotel. It's everything we hoped for," I said.

"Not everything," he responded.

I reached over, patted his hand, but pulled back quickly when I saw how uncomfortable he looked. "You'll be okay, Gerald. I know this isn't ideal for you, but it really will be fine," I said.

He looked at me, his skepticism clear, and then he finally nodded. "I suppose you're right," he said.

"Not suppose. I *am* right," I said.

He laughed. "You are always so emphatic," he said.

"Not always, but I'm right about this," I responded.

"I hope you are. Although…" he said, trailing off.

"What?" I asked, looked at him with concern.

He shrugged. "I guess I'm just tired, but it almost seems like this place is cursed," Gerald said.

"A curse might be too much, but all this stuff that keeps cropping up is a lot to deal with," I responded.

Gerald leaned forward. "You think that's just coincidental?" he asked.

I looked at him curiously. "What do you mean?"

Gerald looked at the door, then looked back at me. "I mean you heard the stories," he said, leaning in even more and whispering.

"What stories, Gerald?" I said, trepidation beginning to take the place of some of the whimsy of earlier.

"The stories. About *them*. You think it's maybe…"

"Gerald, what are you implying?" I asked.

He looked at the door again, then looked back at me. "Nothing. Nothing at all. I'm just a bitter old man, don't pay me any attention," he said.

"Gerald, I—"

The phone rang and I glared at it before I picked it up.

"M. Lounge and Hotel, this is Eden, the assistant general manager, speaking. How may I help you?" I said the familiar lines on autopilot, frustrated at having been interrupted, but grateful for the moment to think about how to approach this with Gerald.

"Eden, it's Shelly. The police are here."

———

EDEN

"Oh my God!"

Less than five minutes after I had left it, I sank back into my chair.

The long days, the problems at the hotel, the conversation with Gerald were all forgotten.

"What happened to them?" I asked when I finally managed to speak.

My eyes had started to water, and tears threatened to fall, but I fought them back, held the gaze of the detective who sat across from me. He looked stoic, not at all shaken by what he had just told me. I guessed he was used to delivering this kind of news.

I just wasn't used to receiving it.

"We found Steve and Bob in an abandoned vehicle, both dead from a single gunshot wound to the head," he said.

"Oh God," I whispered, struggling to wrap my mind around that.

When I looked over at Gerald I saw that his face had gone ashen white—he looked as shocked as I felt.

"Do you know…? When…?" I sputtered.

"Three days is our best guess. We'll know more when we get the coroner's report," he said.

I looked at Gerald again, struggling to comprehend.

"Do you know why?" I asked.

"I was hoping you might have some idea," he responded.

"Me? Why?"

"They used to work for you?" the detective asked.

I nodded quickly. "For years."

"And what happened with their jobs?"

"We had a disagreement about work hours, and I could no longer retain them," I said.

Even through my shock and sadness, I sensed there was an undercurrent in this conversation, something that had nothing to do with Steve and Bob. Instinct told me to tread carefully.

The detective looked around our office, though I couldn't tell if he was simply taking in his surroundings or searching for something particular. "Can you be more specific?" he asked.

I shrugged, trying to be nonchalant, though I was wary. "No. It was nothing of note," I said, not divulging the details, mostly because I sensed there were other motives at play here.

"You sound certain about that," the detective said, looking at me pointedly.

"I am," I replied, stern yet polite. "There are sometimes issues with staff. I'm certain you know how that goes."

By now, the tears that had filled my voice had faded, and I had shifted to my detached, impersonal voice. The detective noticed, and though he gave no outward indication, I was certain he was assessing me.

"Do you know who else they were working for after they left here?" he said.

"No," I replied. "Gerald, do you know?"

Gerald looked at the detective.

"I'm afraid not. I hadn't kept up with them. Eden usually does that kind of thing."

"Is that so?" the detective said.

I looked at Gerald, knowing he hadn't intended it, but still feeling implicated.

I reached into my pocket and retrieved my business card. "Here's my card if you need to contact me. Do their families know?"

"Yeah. I spoke with their wives earlier," the detective replied, taking the card from my hand.

I stood and reached out to shake his hand, still shocked by what he'd told me but more than ready for him to go.

"Thank you for letting us know," I said.

The detective nodded, and I walked him to the parking lot on shaky legs, and then slowly made my way back to my office.

This was unbelievable, and between the shock of their deaths, the strangeness of that conversation with the detective, I was off balance.

"I'm sure you've heard by now," Gerald said as I entered the office.

I instantly saw Michael, and I wanted to throw my arms around him, have him hold me, tell me that everything would be okay.

But I couldn't do that, of course. Besides the fact that doing so would be inappropriate in this environment, I didn't know how he would respond to that, whether he would welcome it.

So instead, I stayed where I was, hovering in the doorway looking between Gerald, who still looked flustered but livelier now that Michael was there, and Michael, whose face showed no expression at all.

"I heard," he said. Then he looked at me. "You okay, Eden?"

I nodded. "I am. It's a shock. We should do something for their families."

"Whatever you think is best," he responded. That was an unusually noncommittal answer from Michael, but I was too preoccupied to examine it too closely or to think about what it might mean.

"Well," Gerald said, clearing his throat, "I'll go gather the department heads and make sure they give the news to the rest of the staff. If they don't already know."

I looked at him. "Thanks, Gerald. And I'll set something up, make sure there's a counselor on hand if anyone needs someone to talk to."

He nodded and then left.

I had stepped aside, but when Gerald was gone I walked into the office, moving intently toward my phone.

Was stopped in my tracks when Michael reached out, wrapped his arms around me.

I let myself rest against him, listening to the thud of his heart under my ear, the steady sound, the warmth of his body calming me.

"You really all right?" he asked, his voice rumbling out of his chest.

Oddly, hearing that question made tears well in my eyes, but I swallowed them back.

"Yeah," I said a long moment later.

Then, using strength I didn't know I had, I pried myself from his arms, went to the phone without looking at him.

I searched the database until I found the phone numbers I'd been looking for.

"I-I need to make a couple of calls," I said, not looking at him.

"Eden," he said.

I kept my gaze down for a moment, then looked up.

"I'll be back in an hour. Then I'll take you home," he said.

"Okay," I said and then I started to dial.

NINETEEN

MICHAEL

I HADN'T WANTED to leave Eden but I needed to talk to Patrick and Declan. We met at Boiler Room but didn't go inside.

"The police have been at the hotel about the guards," I said.

"I'm not surprised. Is this something we should be concerned about?" Patrick asked.

"I don't think so, but I don't know for sure," I said, hating to admit it but not allowing my ego to override common sense.

"You don't know?" Declan said.

"I don't know. After they were fired, I haven't given them a second thought," I said.

"Clearly somebody has," Patrick said.

"Yeah, and I don't like it," I said.

And I didn't. This reflected badly on me. They'd been half-assing it at M. and put Patrick in danger, and now that they were dead, it would bring attention none of us wanted to the family. Two fuckups, ones that Patrick would likely not overlook.

"I'm going to look into this more," I said.

"Why?" Patrick asked.

I studied him, trying to figure out if the question was a test or if he was serious. I couldn't tell, so I simply answered him.

"It's my hotel. I want to know anything there is to know about what's going on in it. I don't want any surprises," I said.

"I agree. But be subtle," Patrick said.

"You say that like you think it's possible," I responded. Patrick had always said I needed a lighter touch. I'd tried, but that clearly had done no good.

"Maybe I'll be surprised," he said.

"Maybe you will," I replied.

Patrick left then, Declan too, and I didn't linger. Instead, I made my way back to the hotel, anxious to see Eden.

She was putting up a good front, but I'd seen

that this news was upsetting to her and I wanted to make her feel better.

Didn't know if I had the capacity to do so, but realized how much I disliked seeing her hurt, especially when there was nothing I could do about it.

I was also grappling with the fact that I cared as much as I did.

There was no way to deny it. I did care.

About her.

About how she felt.

And it was more than sex, which was enough to scare the fuck out of me.

I didn't know if I could manage that, but for now, I'd just be with her, try to get that look out of her eyes.

When I got to the hotel, I looked at the area where I knew Eden parked. I'd told her to park closer, but she'd always refused. Now, her car wasn't there.

That alarmed me, but I ignored it, told myself that she had maybe moved it.

But when I went into the office, found it empty, the truth started to come over me. I still searched the hotel, but I knew it was futile.

Eden was gone.

I told myself to go home, to go anywhere but to her, yet I seemed powerless in the matter. Knowing I had no other choice, I turned the car toward Eden's.

Besides, she needed to explain what she had been thinking. I'd been very specific that I was coming back, and that I had expected her to be there.

That she wasn't was something I wouldn't allow to go unaddressed.

That I'd get to see her, see that she was okay or as okay as she could be, was incidental.

I saw a car parked outside of her house, was relieved that she was there, that relief giving me space to allow anger to the forefront.

I got out and before I reached the front door, she had opened it.

"Michael, I'm a little tired. Can we talk later?" she said, looking weary.

"No," I replied, walking inside.

She looked annoyed, but didn't put up an argument.

Yet another clue that she was not feeling her best.

I stood in her small foyer, looking at the place, feeling comfortable here.

That was what Eden did. She made people feel comfortable, feel better. That I felt that way at her home was no surprise, was in fact, something worth celebrating.

"I told you I was coming back," I said when Eden closed the door.

"I..." She trailed off, looked down and then back up at me.

"What is it?" I asked, sounding more impatient than I felt. When she didn't respond, I softened my voice. "Are you really okay?"

"I think so," she said, sounding uncertain, tentative. Not at all like Eden.

"Did you speak to their families?" I asked.

She nodded quickly. "I told them M. would take care of arrangements," she said. Her brows dropped low and her eyes darkened more.

"And?" I asked, knowing there was something more to this.

"They said no. Told me that they'd had more than enough of your family's dirty money," she said.

After she spoke, she looked at me, clearly gauging my reaction.

I shrugged. "Their loss."

Eden clearly didn't like that reaction. She frowned.

"Does it bother you that it doesn't bother me?" I asked.

"Shouldn't it bother you?" she tossed back.

Not an answer, but I decided to indulge her.

"Why? Too bad for those guys that they're dead, but if their wives don't see or don't want to take what I'm offering, it's no skin off my ass," I said, meaning it.

"And the other?" she asked.

"What other?" I responded.

She looked at me, sighed. "I think you know what I mean, Michael," she whispered.

I reached up and grabbed her chin, tilted her head until her eyes locked with mine.

"Why don't you explain it to me?" I asked, ignoring how happy I was to be touching her again, even under these circumstances.

"The part about dirty money. That doesn't bother you?"

"No."

"You mean that, don't you?" she asked.

"I do. Everything in my hotel is clean. You should know that better than anyone. You should know that despite what others might say," I said.

"And everything else?" she asked.

"Eden," I said, my eyes not leaving hers, "what are you asking me?"

"I..." She trailed off, looked down, looked up again. "I don't know," she finally said.

"I don't believe you," I responded.

"Questioning my word again, Mr. Murphy?" she whispered, a smile in her voice.

"I am. Now tell me, what are you asking me?"

This was dangerous territory. Unprecedented territory. Eden and I were circling around the topic I never wished to discuss. One I *wouldn't* discuss with her or anyone else who wasn't a Murphy.

She looked at me, her eyes dark, her face pinched.

"A detective came to the hotel," she said.

"I know. About Steve and Bob," I said.

She chuckled humorlessly. "Why am I not surprised you know that? You did warn me you know what happens in your hotel," she said.

"I do," I responded, ignoring the fact that I hadn't known about Steve and Bob.

Eden broke away then, and I found that I

missed even that tenuous connection with her. But, despite my instincts, I didn't press further, didn't try to get her to open up to me.

I had naively thought I would avoid this conversation, even hoped that it wouldn't matter. Foolishly, I thought that once I got Eden out of my system, it wouldn't matter.

I had been incredibly wrong.

She was in my system, deep, and that made this conversation an inevitability.

The inevitability didn't make it comfortable, and certainly didn't give me any guidance as to how to handle it.

I would have to ask Patrick.

"Eden, ask your question," I said, steeling myself for what she would say.

She had turned, but then she turned back, looked at me.

"Michael, are the things they say about you, about your family, true?" she whispered.

I had known the words were coming, and yet I wasn't prepared for them and I didn't know how to answer them. I'd never been ashamed of my family or what we did. It was simply a part of me, something I couldn't change. Something I didn't want to.

But when I looked at Eden now, I realized that

as much as I couldn't change who I was, what she thought of me mattered. For a fleeting moment, I wondered what it would be like to give her a simple answer, say that I was a dedicated business owner like that asshole Kevin and nothing more.

But I couldn't say that, and I wouldn't lie.

So I kissed her.

After she broke the kiss, she looked at me.

"Michael, this doesn't solve everything," she said.

"No. Not everything. But for now…"

Instead of finishing, I kissed her again.

At first, she was still, but soon she softened in my arms, yielding to me. I pulled her close to me, deepened the kiss. Only broke it long enough to follow her to her bedroom.

It was funny but this didn't feel strange at all. This was only my second time in her home, but it felt like I was where I was supposed to be, where I belonged. Some part of me suspected that anywhere with Eden was where I belonged.

I kissed her once more and then broke away, moved slowly as I removed her clothes.

I admired her for a moment, her body beckoning me, but even more, the softly glazed look in her eye making me happy because at least in this moment I could comfort her. I followed suit, making quick work of my own clothes, pausing only long enough to slide on a condom.

I laid Eden down gently, and then began kissing her, moving down the smooth skin on her neck, down her full, dark-tipped breasts, teasing one bud until it stood taut and then moving to the other.

As I kissed her, I slid my hands down the soft expanse of her stomach, cupped her warm, wet sex in my hands.

Like always, feeling her heat, knowing that I would soon be inside her set my blood on fire, but I moved slow, didn't rush as I stroked her until she moaned.

"Michael, please," she whimpered.

Hearing her did something to me, almost broke my control, but I kept it and didn't give in to the mad desire to take her.

Instead, I pushed inside her slowly, filling her inch by inch as our mingled breaths filled the room.

When I was fully seated I paused, enjoying the sensation of her around me, beneath me.

Then I opened my eyes.

When I met hers, I knew I was lost.

TWENTY

MICHAEL

Once Eden was sleeping, I left her again, headed unerringly in one direction.

When I got to Patrick's, I found him up and in his study.

"You never sleep," I said.

"No," he responded. "What happened?"

"I…" I trailed off, looked at him, wondering why the hell I was even doing this.

"This isn't about business," Patrick said, the words a statement and not a question.

"Not entirely, I guess," I said, not yet able to say out loud what I suspected in my heart.

"So tell me," he said.

"When you and Nya…" I paused, again considering how best to frame the words. "When you and Nya hooked up, how did you handle it?"

"I assume you're asking about how I handled Nya and the business?" he said.

"Yeah," I replied.

"I was lucky in some sense I guess. Our circumstances left little doubt as to what she was dealing with. So the rest kind of took care of itself," he responded.

"That's no fucking help at all, Patrick," I said.

He smiled. "Guess not. I assume this isn't a hypothetical question that brings you here at this hour?"

"No. Not hypothetical," I whispered.

"I also assume that you're still screwing around with my assistant general manager?" he said.

"She's *our* assistant general manager," I responded.

"Michael, what the fuck are you doing with her?" Patrick asked, his voice serious.

"What do you mean?" I asked.

"Eden's good. I'd hate for you to screw things up with her," Patrick said.

"What about me? You aren't worried about me getting screwed up?" I said.

Patrick shrugged. "I have two other brothers. A

replacement for Eden is going to be harder to come by," he said.

"Thanks, Pat," I responded, but had to laugh.

He smiled, then circled his desk to sit next to me.

"So, you asking this question tells me that this thing with Eden isn't just some fling," he said.

"I don't know what the fuck it is," I replied, frustrated.

"We seldom do, until we do," Patrick said.

"Yeah, whatever, but if something comes from this, and that's a big fucking if, how am I supposed to handle it?"

"I don't know, Michael, but I'll say this. Eden's not stupid. If she's involved with you, she has to have some idea of what she's getting into."

"So what, I just leave it to chance?"

"Honestly, I don't want you talking about this with her at all," he said.

"Trust me, I don't plan to, but she deserves an answer before this goes too far," I said, for the first time acknowledging that this thing with Eden might be more than I let on, even to myself.

"If she's meant for you, nothing else will matter," he said.

"Easy as that, huh?" I said, looking at him skeptically.

"Yes," he replied with certainty.

———

EDEN

I'd been sad to see Michael go last night, but was also happy that I had a little space, a little distance. I needed it, needed some room to think, try to understand what was happening.

I still felt terrible about Steve and Bob, but I felt closer to Michael.

I shouldn't have, though.

He had been careful with his words last night, but I knew that even if all the whispers weren't true in their details, Michael and his brothers were criminals.

And I knew I didn't care.

Maybe I was wrong, maybe it was something I would come to regret, but it didn't matter to me. What the Murphys did, what Michael did, was completely secondary to who he was. And last night as he had held me, I felt more at home, more at peace than I ever had before.

Just my luck that it would be with him, but I'd learn to manage. Michael was worth it.

When I heard the phone ringing, I moved quickly to my desk.

"It's me, Eden," Shelly said.

"What's up, Shelly?" I asked, smiling at the sound of her voice.

"Kevin Carson is here," she said.

"Tell him I'll be right out," I responded.

I had no plans to meet Kevin, but I was certain he had come by after he heard about Steve and Bob. They had worked together for a couple of years, and I thought it was quite nice of him to come by.

"Hey, Kevin," I said as I approached.

He reached for me, hugged me quickly and then looked down.

"Eden, I heard what happened," he said as he stared at me, his expression concerned.

"Yeah, it's a shame," I said, starting to tear up.

Kevin reached for me, seemingly to touch my cheek.

"What the fuck are you doing here?"

TWENTY-ONE

MICHAEL

I ignored Eden and focused on Kevin and the way he stood so close to her and the way he touched her like he had every right to.

Eden didn't seem eager to pull away, something I would address with her later. After I handled him.

Kevin looked at Eden, the emotion clear on his face. Then he looked at me, daring, the challenge clear.

"Kevin and I were—"

"I wasn't talking to you, Eden."

The tone of my voice left no doubt as to my seriousness, but to my surprise, Eden stayed quiet. I could only imagine what I must look like, the energy I had to be giving off for her to say nothing.

Then I realized it must have been much worse

when Kevin shifted to put himself between her and me. My rage, already blinding, went up yet another notch.

"Eden and I were having a conversation," he said, looking into my eyes without blinking.

"You and Eden have nothing to discuss," I said, my voice certain, not giving any hint about the fact that I wasn't.

"Doesn't she get to decide that?" he asked.

"No," I replied flatly.

"Wait just a damn minute," Eden interrupted.

"I told you I wasn't talking to you, Eden," I said without looking at her, "so shut up."

"Don't talk to her like that," Kevin said.

The rage that had been cooking boiled over. I moved without thinking, my fist connecting with his face.

I hit him so hard, I could feel sharp pains in my wrist.

To his credit, Kevin didn't drop.

Instead, he stood for a moment, stunned, and then charged, leveling his shoulder into my chest and driving me backward.

I reacted instantly, landing as many blows to his body as I could, not even stopping when I landed against the solid wall.

I heard Eden scream, but didn't spare a moment to look at her. I was too focused on this, happy to have some outlet for the anger nearly blinding me.

This, this I understood, could handle. What Eden made me feel, feelings at all, were something I didn't want, something I had no desire to try to understand.

But this…

I hit Kevin as hard as I could, a blow he returned in kind, his fist connecting with my ribs.

That would hurt like hell tomorrow, but I didn't care. The pain was worth it if only for the solace that the physical combat brought.

"What the fuck!"

I looked up when I heard the familiar voice, looked away when I heard Kevin swing. I ducked and then threw another punch, landing against Kevin's jaw and following up with a left that landed on his side.

We were on the ground grappling, and I could only imagine how we must look, but I didn't care. Kevin slipped away, so I got up and went for him. I continued to swing, was stopped by Declan's iron grip on my hand.

I tried to shake him off, keep moving, but he twisted my arm behind my back.

I could have kept going, but at this angle, Declan's hold would have broken my arm, and he probably wouldn't give a shit.

So I stayed still, looked at Kevin as he started to charge.

"I wouldn't do that," Declan said.

The lethal calmness of his voice seemed to penetrate the rage I could see on Kevin's face.

He slowed, then came to a stop, bending over and breathing hard, blood dripping from his nose.

"I don't know who you are, but you need to get the fuck out of here," Declan said.

"We have unfinished business," Kevin said around a heavily exhaled breath.

"Do you want me to finish it?" Declan said.

He went silent then, staring at Kevin, who stared at me with malice in his eyes. "Later, Murphy," he said.

"Fuck you," I replied.

Declan added a little twist to his hold, one that cut my words off with a sharp sting of pain. He didn't release it as Kevin left, the elevator doors swishing shut with finality.

"I should break your fucking arm," Declan said through clenched teeth.

"Do it or don't, but let me go," I said.

He twisted a little bit more and then released me.

I stood, took a few moments to adjust my shirt and jacket, and then looked at Eden.

The scorn in her eyes was apparent, stony with its intensity.

I waited for her to speak. She didn't though. Instead she looked at me, her eyes alight with something like hate.

She looked at Declan. "Thank you," she said.

Then, she turned, rounded the corner without looking back.

The few seconds of comfort I'd found in beating up Kevin were gone in an instant.

Now, all I had was a faint hint of sadness because Eden was gone. I was left with a brother who looked like he wanted to finish the job Kevin had started.

"What the fuck is wrong with you, Michael?"

"Not now, Declan."

"Now," he said, slamming me in the shoulder.

I looked at him, eyes clashing with his, and was again reminded of how much like Patrick he looked.

And much like Patrick did most of the time, he looked like he wanted to kick my face in.

That was unusual for Declan. He never took sides in whatever squabbles between us there might be. He was also slow to anger, but right now, he was pissed.

"This is what you call running the hotel?" he said.

"I told you I'm in no mood," I said, waving him off, torn between frustration that he had interrupted and shame that Eden had seen me lose control so completely.

"And I told you I don't give a fuck. Go change and get to the garage. I will make sure that none of your employees saw you acting like a fucking idiot in the middle of *our* business," he said.

"What do you want, Declan?" I said, glaring at him.

"Garage in ten minutes, Michael. Don't make me come look for you," he said.

Then he turned, stormed off, no doubt in search of Eden, ready to do the damage control that was my responsibility.

I knew how messed up that was, but Declan needed to see my point. That asshole had no business being in my hotel like he had a right to be there, touching Eden like he had the right to.

He didn't, and if he hadn't grasped that yet, I'd be happy to explain it again.

I headed toward my office, my face tight, expression, I knew, fierce. I'd never asked Eden about the nature of her relationship with Kevin, but those few seconds had been enough for me to see what Kevin wanted from Eden, and it had nothing to do with catching up on old times.

My stomach churned with anger as I remembered those seconds, the way Eden had seemed to be enjoying his attention.

I had no doubt that was what had me so on edge.

Eden liked fucking me, maybe almost as much as I liked fucking her. I had no doubt about that, but it went no further than that. I'd gone to Patrick, considered how to invite Eden into parts of my life I shared with no one.

For nothing.

She never looked at me with softness in her eyes, didn't seem happy to see me in the way she had him.

That fucking hurt. And I fucking hated it.

Hated that she felt, or rather, didn't feel that way about me.

Hated that I cared, that I was powerless not to.

Hated knowing that if forced to choose, she wouldn't choose me.

I had no claim on her, had no right to want such a thing, but I didn't care. Because I did want her. I might not be able to keep her, but there was no fucking way I would let that dick Kevin be the reason.

Yeah, Michael, you can get rid of her yourself. Push her away. You've done it before.

I ignored that thought and the truth that was attached to it, and changed into jeans and a T-shirt, then tossed my suit in the garbage. It was ripped, and I didn't want the hassle of having it repaired or the memory of what had damaged it in the first place.

I was in the garage in eight minutes, and Declan was waiting for me. He was still tense but seemed a little bit calmer than he had before, his massive arms crossed over his chest but his face was blank, impassive.

"Get in," he said.

My first instinct was to ask why, but I ignored it, and instead rounded the vehicle and got into the passenger side.

I didn't say a word as Declan drove off, knew

that doing so would be the first sign of defeat in this little battle of wills.

Besides, I could guess at what he would say. Probably have some bullshit lecture about how I needed to listen to Patrick, be more laid-back, do as I was told.

All shit I'd heard a million times, all shit I had no interest in.

Declan drove for about twenty minutes, the silence in the interior of the car an almost tangible thing.

He slowed to a stop in front of an abandoned warehouse, then turned to look at me.

I looked back at him, waiting.

"You really are that fucking stupid?" he said.

"Probably, since I have no idea what you're talking about," I said truthfully.

"No, you don't. Always going on and on about your rightful place in the family, and you can't control yourself long enough not to fight in the fucking hallway in front of security cameras."

He shook his head and I scowled.

"I don't get what the big fucking deal is."

"Of course not, Michael. You don't get it because you're an idiot and a baby," Declan said, his voice raised as high as I had heard it in years. He glared at me, his breath coming out on hard exhales.

"Do you know why I brought you here?"

"I assume to insult me," I replied.

"Very fucking funny. I went to Patrick and talked to him."

"About what?" I said.

"The weather," he spat, glaring hard. "What the fuck do you think?"

"Declan, get to the point," I said, too distracted to think about what Declan was saying when my mind was on Eden.

"The point is, Michael, I convinced Patrick, against his better judgment, he needed to cut you a break and start giving you some real responsibility. And what do I find after I do that? You, acting like a jerk-off for the whole world to see. What did that guy do anyway?"

"Why does it matter?" I said, annoyed that Declan was questioning me, even more pissed at myself for the answer.

Declan glared at me, his jaw ticking now.

"He was getting a little too familiar with Eden," I said.

Declan lifted a brow. "Did he touch her?"

"No. Not exactly. It…"

I trailed off, looked at Declan as I saw the dawning realization.

He gave me something akin to a smile and then shook his head.

"I should have known," he said.

His voice still held a measure of disgust but it was dampened by amusement.

I didn't share the feeling, not when I was once again proving to someone else what I had so long denied to myself.

"It's not important. Why am I here?"

"I guess I can appreciate the situation," Declan said. "But next time, try talking to the woman and not attacking someone who just so happens to be standing in the same room with her."

"He was trying to do more than that," I said, only hearing my own tone of voice after I spoke the words.

"Whatever it was," Declan said, serious again, "you have responsibilities, a reputation to maintain at the hotel and elsewhere. I don't care how pissed off you are. You just can't go around knocking out whoever the fuck you feel like."

"It worked for Aengus," I said.

"Did it?" Declan replied.

I said nothing, knowing I didn't have a leg to

stand on. As far as I could see, Aengus lived a shitty life, one no one should be jealous of.

Declan knew it. I did too.

"So why am I here?" I asked yet again.

"Patrick wants to give you a chance—there's a matter inside that needs to be taken care of," he said.

I looked at him, my mind going back to that day all those years ago.

"What is it?" I said.

"A former employee who likes to take things that don't belong to him," Declan said.

"What am I supposed to do about it?" I asked, excited but also wondering what the catch was.

Declan locked eyes with me. "That's for you to decide."

He unlocked the door, and even though he didn't speak, I knew it was my sign to get out.

I did and walked slowly toward the warehouse, considering.

As I got further away from the SUV, I looked back for a moment and watched as Declan reversed and then drove away.

This was a test.

Even before Declan had left, I knew that.

The question was, would I fail it?

TWENTY-TWO

MICHAEL

When I entered, I saw a lone figure sitting in the chair in the middle of the room. I walked toward him, realized I recognized him when I got close.

It was Arnold Greer, a long-standing employee, for lack of a better word, the one who was charged with making sure the books stayed accurate and that everyone who came to the Murphys for our services was accounted for.

I was surprised he'd ended up in this position, but then tried to remind myself I shouldn't be. He wasn't family, so he shouldn't have been trusted.

"Arnold," I said.

"Michael," he replied.

His voice was calm, but his eyes were red and

puffy, and I could see the track of tears that stained his cheeks.

"What happened?" I asked when I came to a stop in front of him.

I'd seen Patrick ask that same question more times than I could remember, and before I had thought it was a simple courtesy, a chance to have a man say his piece.

But now, I realized it wasn't.

I was interested in what Arnold had to say and hadn't yet decided what I'd do. What had gotten him here had been bad, but that he still lived told me that there was some room for interpretation as there had been when Patrick had asked that question, something he'd clearly intended for me to see.

I looked at Arnold, trying to read his expression.

"It's…unfortunate," he said.

"That it is, Arnold," I replied. "What happened?"

I was surprisingly calm, my voice not reflecting anything I felt inside.

Inside, I was a mix of emotions, excited that Patrick had decided to trust me, eager to prove to him that he'd been right to do so, and most of all, determined to give Arnold a fair hearing.

He shrugged. "I got into a bind. Did something stupid."

"How long were you stealing from us?" I asked.

I was curious about his answer, more surprised than I should have been he was here. Besides the fact that Arnold was compensated quite well, he and Patrick had a good relationship, and if Arnold had gotten into a bind, Patrick would have helped him.

Any of my brothers would have.

"I have a wife, two mistresses. It gets expensive," he said.

Arnold looked up at me then, smiled, and I returned the expression. "Maybe two is too many," I replied. It seemed beyond stupid that Arnold had allowed himself to get into this kind of position over pussy, but that had been his choice to make.

"Hindsight being what it is, I tend to agree," he said.

"So it has come to this," I said.

"It has. But that I'm alive suggests to me that I have a chance. Is that true?"

"It's true," I said.

"Then I won't tell you how sorry I am, and I won't beg for my life. I'll just promise you I won't do this again," he said.

"I appreciate that, Arnold," I said, though I regretted he hadn't thought of that before he acted.

I met his eyes and waited.

"So where does that leave us?" he asked.

I studied Arnold as I considered the lifetime that had led to this moment, the one I would live after it.

"Where indeed," I whispered.

TWENTY-THREE

EDEN

It was nearly midnight when I calmed down enough to even consider going to bed.

For hours I had replayed those moments, thought about how angry I was at Michael. He had no right to behave the way he had. And her certainly had no right to tell me to shut up.

He was a fucking asshole, something I'd known for years, but this should have been the thing to finally get it through my head.

So what that Kevin had been intent on using a tragedy to his advantage? He hadn't crossed any of the lines Michael had, repeatedly, and if he had, I knew without a doubt I would have put him in his place.

Not Michael, though.

I didn't recognize the doormat I became when Michael was around, still didn't know what about him made me lose myself.

But the reasons didn't matter.

What mattered was that I couldn't allow this to continue to happen, wouldn't let Michael walk all over me.

As much as I might have wished it otherwise, as addicted to him as I was, I would end...whatever it was between us if he couldn't accept that.

My heart clenched at the thought, but I ignored it, just as I ignored the suspicion that Michael wouldn't accept what I had to say. Nothing I had ever seen of him told me that he would, so if I were smart, I'd get on with the business of trying to forget about him, of trying to forget about the way that he, and only he, made me feel.

Because as much as I loved that feeling, craved it, I loved and respected myself more.

The problem was, I didn't trust myself, not when it came to Michael. So I would have to stand firm. I would not yield on this.

I thought about calling Kevin again to check on him, but the four other calls I had placed earlier had gone unanswered. He'd seemed mostly unhurt, though explosively pissed when he'd left the hotel, and I guess I couldn't blame him if he didn't want to talk to me.

Still, I felt some measure of responsibility, chided myself for doing so.

Michael was an adult, responsible for his own actions, just as I was mine.

Rather than spend one of my days off thinking about him, I would rest, plan what I wanted to do with my free time, and forget about Michael, Kevin, and M. Lounge and Hotel for the moment.

No sooner had I decided that than the doorbell rang. I knew exactly who it was. No one else would show up at this hour without so much as a call.

My anger intensified, chased by incredulity.

He couldn't possibly be showing up here, now, not after the way he'd behaved.

I jammed my feet into my slippers, not slowing long enough to grab a robe as I went to the door.

Everything inside of me knew what awaited me on the other side of the door, and beyond the shock of him having the gall to come here now, there was some excitement about the fact that I wouldn't have to wait to tell Michael exactly what I thought about him and where he could stick his macho bullshit.

The words were already formed, hovering on the

tip of my tongue, waiting to explode out of me when I pulled the door open.

And they died there when I took a look at him.

He was dressed down, as casual as I'd ever seen him, but it wasn't his clothes that made the difference.

It was his demeanor, the unfamiliar aura that hung around him.

He looked like Michael, his face unsmiling, looking as though it was ready to turn into a frown at any moment, his eyes alert. But where I was so used to seeing anger in them, was used to him always being prepared to fight, I didn't see that this time.

He looked tired. A word I never associated with Michael, one I decided I didn't like.

"Come in," I said, closing the door behind him after he entered.

I turned, looked at him, and waited.

Waited some more. And then, in the next breath he reached for me and crushed me into a tight embrace.

It was unlike any other we had ever shared.

The thrill of being close to him, feeling his arms around me, his body against mine was still there, but there was a depth now, a difference.

There was emotion.

Michael held me like he never wanted to let me go. And I let him, held him back, hoping he wouldn't.

After a while, he dropped his arms, looked at me in the eyes.

I still wasn't sure what was happening, but following my instincts, I reached up, touched his face.

"You want to talk about it?" I asked, my eyes searching his.

"No," he said.

"Then let's go to bed," I said.

I lowered my hand, reached for his, and led him to my bedroom.

He knew the way, but when we got there, instead of the explosive passion, the combustible chemistry that had been there, Michael lay beside me.

As I drifted to sleep, I realized this was the most intimate moment I'd ever shared with anyone.

———

EDEN

The next morning was the culmination of more dreams than I could even count at this point.

The number of times I had closed my eyes, imagined what it would be like to wake up with Michael Murphy in my bed were numerous, embarrassingly frequent.

And nothing compared to the reality of him being there.

When I awoke, I'd stayed there frozen, what had happened the night before all coming back to me in a flash.

When it did, I was troubled, but even more I was happy.

Because sometime during the night, Michael had wrapped his arms around me, pulled me against the solid wall of his chest. Now I was caged by him, surrounded by the warmth of his body, the strength in his arms, the unique scent that was so Michael.

His breathing told me that he was awake, but I didn't speak, didn't even move.

We had things to deal with, and we would, but for now, I wanted to steal this moment, take it while I had it.

So I did, lay there, my eyes sealed shut though I could see the sunlight behind them.

I didn't even move at the first brush of Michael's lips against my shoulder.

Didn't move when he brushed his lips against my neck, then down, leaving a trail of kisses between my shoulder blades, tracing my spine down, down.

As his lips moved down, his hand moved up, starting at my knee, up my thigh, settling against my mound.

I moved then, the tremors that rocked my body growing more intense as he kissed me, smoothed his hands over me.

I arched my back, pushing my hips until they were flush against his body, his burgeoning hardness nestling between my ass cheeks. I rocked against him, needy, desperate for more, was rewarded by a little jerk of Michael's cock.

He had been tracing his fingers in an irregular pattern over my skin, but when I rocked once more, he moved his hands forward, trailed them down, swirling his fingertips in the coarse hair of my sex, using that same slow, swirling motion to move his fingers along the delicate skin of my inner thigh before he settled at my center.

Like always, I was wet for him, ready, and like always, he took what I so freely offered, dipping one finger, then a second into my wetness, still moving in those slow, lazy swirls, circling his finger around, and round.

I was taut with need, everything around me fading as Michael kissed my spine, his breath warm against me as he pressed his lips at the small of my back and then began working his way up again.

I was almost swept away in my own world but not so much that I missed the way his breath hitched, the way he tightened the hold he had around my waist. I sighed my disappointment when he broke away, but went quiet when he shifted until he lay on his side, his strong arm locked around my waist, his cock, heavy, hard between my thighs.

More than anything, I wanted him to enter me, was anxious to feel the way he would spread me, the way my walls would pulse around his thickness.

But he didn't, something I knew I would be grateful for later, but now I resented it. At least I did until he thrust, sent his hips lurching forward until his cockhead hit my clit.

The reverberating sensation was sheer pleasure, almost overwhelming in its strength.

When he did so again, I cried out, squeezing my thighs closed tighter as he pistoned his hips. He breathed out a harsh breath, began to move faster.

Wetness was running from me freely, coating the inside of my thighs, his shaft, both of us now sticky.

I didn't care.

He wasn't even inside me, but I was ready to explode, the *tap tap tap* of his cock against my clit driving me insane.

So mindless that I didn't care about the bright sun that filled my room, leaving no possibility he couldn't see the sag of my breasts, the fullness of my thighs, the paunch of my stomach.

I'd never been so exposed in front of Michael in the daylight, and before had been nervous about what would happen when I was, how he would respond. There was no way he could miss any of them now, but he seemed not to care. He slammed his lean, strong hips into mine, centered his hand on that paunch to hold me in place.

When he tightened his hand, hit my clit one last time, I cried out, lost myself in an intense climax, one that left me shivering, shattered.

A moment later, he spilled himself, his cum painting my thighs as he exhaled hard. My sweat, our combined juices on my skin, Michael's tight hold on my waist, his harsh breath against my ear couldn't detract from the beauty of this moment.

I still hadn't opened my eyes, but reached for Michael when I felt him move.

"Stay still," he whispered.

I didn't defy him but instead lay there, listened to the sound of him moving in my bathroom and then his footsteps as he approached.

I sighed at the first feel of the warm cloth against my legs, shifted to give him access as he wiped away his essence. It was insane, but I was saddened that he was no longer there and at the same time flattered by his thoughtfulness.

This was how I had imagined it, Michael, gentle, kind, but still him, me as content as I could ever recall being.

But as beautiful as this moment was, I knew it was short-lived.

I kept my eyes closed as long as I could, waited, and then finally turned to face him.

His jaw was shadowed, stubble peppering it, and his hair, usually so neat was unruly.

I found myself reaching for the dark strands, pushing them back away from his forehead, letting my fingers move over his rough jaw, down the bare expanse of his chest.

It blew my mind that he was here, left me somewhat off balance that he even wanted me. I hated myself for thinking that, knew that I deserved no less, and again began remembering what had happened the night before.

I looked at Michael, could see the subtle change in his expression, knew he was aware of the direction my thoughts had taken.

"Get dressed. Then we'll talk," he said.

There was Michael. Always issuing orders.

This time, I complied. I didn't want to give in to him, felt compelled to prove a point. Even more, I knew he was right. We needed to talk.

So instead of staring at Michael's beauty, thinking of how thoroughly he had mastered my body or how much he pissed me off, I got up, dressed quickly in casual clothes and left Michael in my bedroom, went to my kitchen to wait for him.

He emerged a few minutes later, casually taking in my home.

It gave me some measure of shame that I had let Michael fuck me in public, and at my workplace, but he'd never actually seen my kitchen.

Another sign of how out of control I had let things get, how I had lost myself.

No more.

"I have some things to say to you, Michael," I said.

He stood, arms hanging at his side, the tilt of his head still arrogant, but a softness in his eyes I didn't always see.

He nodded curtly.

"What you did yesterday was way out of line. You don't get to go around hitting people. And you sure as shit don't get to tell me to shut up," I said.

Even thinking it now, I felt some of that anger returning. Mostly at myself. Because despite what I'd resolved, I had welcomed him with open arms, had again given myself to him with no hesitation.

That probably made my words now seem weak, meaningless, something I knew Michael wouldn't miss, something I knew he would probably take advantage of.

Because I could keep my firm line, tell him what was and was not acceptable, but the truth was, I had no idea if I could hold that line. Didn't know that I wouldn't spread my legs in the middle of the hotel lobby if Michael crooked his finger.

Pathetic. And what a place to be. At Michael Murphy's mercy.

After I spoke, I continued to look at him, kept me eyes on him as I waited, trying to anticipate what he might say.

"Okay," he finally said.

"I don't think you understood what…" I started and then trailed off quickly, looking at him quizzically. "Okay?"

"Yeah."

Talk about taking the wind out of my sails.

Michael had just agreed with me, hadn't put up any kind of argument at all.

The question was, why wasn't I happier about it?

TWENTY-FOUR

MICHAEL

Leaving Eden's that morning was one of the hardest things I had ever done, but it was much easier than the alternative.

Because the alternative would have been staying there telling her I didn't want to go, and that was something I could not do.

Yesterday, Patrick had finally given me a chance, one that had put me on the road I wanted to be on.

Had I been happy about it?

No.

Instead of focusing on what that chance meant, I'd been intent on getting to her, desperate, needy to be close to her again.

And when she had opened the door, her face

angry, her eyes sparking, I had felt a relief unlike any before.

When she'd held me in her arms with no question, no hesitation, I had once again realized this woman held my heart. I fucking hated it.

I had ignored the signs before, had pretended that it was all normal, that all this was just a fuck to blow off steam, a method of proving to Eden that she wasn't as immune to me as she liked to pretend.

Last night had finally, irrevocably, proven that was a lie.

Because the sex was good, better than good. And Eden was funny, smart, admirable.

I loved her.

Acknowledging that, even only to myself was a punch in the gut. I almost couldn't believe I'd admitted it. But I had, and it was true.

I just had no damn clue what to do with that emotion.

A good man, a decent one would have just cut her loose.

I wasn't good, decent, and I certainly wouldn't let her go.

I couldn't.

But that left me in an awful bind.

Because as unacceptable as it was to think of

someone else having her, I wasn't sure that I could give Eden what she wanted, what she deserved. Maybe she could accept what I did, but even then, would that be enough? Or would she decide I was too difficult a person to be worth the hassle?

I didn't know the answer to that question, and that uncertainty left me in a place that I swore I never would be again.

My stomach churned as I thought of that, yet another problem for me to untangle.

I wouldn't be able to untangle it now, I realized as I turned down the long driveway to the house Patrick lived in permanently. It belonged to all of us, a gift from our mother, but Patrick and his wife, Nya, lived here, and though we were always welcome, we tried to give them space.

On this Sunday morning, I couldn't wait. I parked, went into the house, and found Patrick in the study.

"Where's Nya?" I asked without preamble as I settled in the chair across from Patrick's desk.

"Good morning, Michael. Nya is with her friend Jade. Are you keeping track of my wife's whereabouts?" he asked.

"We need to talk," I said.

Instantly he turned serious, nodded toward the

door. I closed it, then returned to sit across from him.

"Have you talked to Declan?" I asked.

"He told me he gave you a job last night," Patrick said.

"Is that all he said?"

"Yes. Was there something else?" Patrick asked.

That was like Declan. He knew I would tell Patrick what happened, and so I did.

"I got into a little scuffle at the hotel," I said.

"A scuffle?" Patrick said. His expression was inscrutable as usual, but I thought I saw some amusement.

"Someone Eden used to know. He got familiar," I said.

"Did he touch her?" Patrick asked.

He was mirroring Declan's question, and as I had last night, I gave the same answer.

"It wasn't that. It was just a…misunderstanding," I said.

"Misunderstanding, meaning you went off half-cocked and tried to beat some asshole half to death because he touched what you think is yours?" Patrick said.

Having him lay it out in such dry terms put my

actions in a different light. Maybe I had overreacted, but I couldn't change that now. Honestly, as long as it hadn't ruined things with Eden, I didn't care.

"I didn't come here to talk about that, Patrick," I said, my usual impatience at bay with the other things on my mind.

"So I'm right. What did you come here to talk about?" he said, going from joking to business in the blink of an eye.

"That task you gave me last night. Was it a test?"

"What makes you think it was a test?"

"Don't bullshit me, Pat. I know it was a test," I said.

"I'm not bullshitting you, Michael, I'm asking you a question. Why do you think it's a test?"

"What else would it be!" I said.

I lowered my voice when I saw the surprise on Patrick's face, but that didn't do anything to temper my anger. It didn't touch me, didn't do anything to stem the tide of my emotions.

"Is that something Aengus taught you?" I spat.

"Michael, I don't know what you're talking about, but you need to calm down and explain," he said.

"It's fucking bullshit that you did that, Patrick," I said, not really hearing anything he said.

"Michael," Patrick whispered, standing, his voice firm, "what is it?"

He circled the desk and walked toward me, putting his hand on my shoulder.

I looked at him, saw the pure confusion in his face.

"Arnold's dead," I said flatly. I'd practiced my explanation in my head, intended to explain to Patrick that I had no choice. Arnold had stolen from us to cover his lies. A man who would cheat on his wife and both of his mistresses couldn't be trusted.

But I didn't have the chance.

"Okay," Patrick responded.

"Okay?" I asked, wondering what else he would say.

"Yeah. Okay," he replied.

I looked at him, confused. "So did I fail?"

"Michael," he said, his eyes locked on mine, "I don't know what you're talking about."

"Did you put me in that situation to see what I would do?"

Patrick frowned deeper, his brows drooping.

"Of course not. I said the choice was yours and I meant it."

He sounded so sincere, and I had never known Patrick to lie, but this was hard to believe. Could I hope that Patrick trusted me so much, so unconditionally? "You mean it?" I asked, hating how hopeful I sounded, but feeling it nonetheless.

"I don't know what this is about, Michael," he said.

"It's nothing. Just some shit with Aengus," I said, sinking back down into my chair, feeling weak.

"You have to be more specific," Patrick said, sitting beside me.

I looked at him, debating what to say, whether to say anything at all. Then, finally, I decided to. "So he didn't test you?" I finally said.

"Undoubtedly, but you really need to be more specific," he said.

I went quiet for a moment, looked out of the window at the peaceful yard, thinking back all those years. I'd never shared this with anyone, not even Sean, but even after all this time, the shame that filled me made me weak.

When I looked at Patrick, I saw his steadiness, was again reminded that he was the leader of this family in a way Aengus could never dream of.

"You were out of the house by then," I started, then paused when Patrick narrowed his eyes, already angry.

That had been a tough time, one when Patrick and Declan had been gone, leaving only me and Sean. It hadn't been long. Patrick had gotten us soon after, but that year with Aengus had been the worst of my life.

"It was my birthday, my twelfth. Aengus left Sean at home and told me to come with him," I said.

"What the fuck did he do?" Patrick asked through clenched teeth.

"He said it was time to prove that I was a man," I said, thinking back on that day.

"I don't exactly remember where we went, but there was a man there, a kid really. Aengus said he had been stealing, said that as a Murphy I could never let something like that stand."

"He made you kill the guy," Patrick said, his voice grim.

"He wanted me to. He even handed me the gun, but I couldn't pull the trigger."

I remembered that day so vividly, the weight of the gun in my hand, the way I had wanted to throw

up, the sound of Aengus's laughter after the first tear
had slipped from my eye.

"We were there for over an hour I think. Every
second was awful. He was taunting me. Telling me I
would never be a real man, said I was a pussy. Soft."

"That piece of shit," Patrick muttered, his expression angry, but at least he didn't look sympathetic.

"He got impatient, took the gun and shot the
kid. I can still hear that sound, feel the droplets of
blood as they splashed against my face," I said.

I'd been terrified then, felt sorry for that kid,
afraid of Aengus. But now, for the first time, I felt
sorry for the boy I had been, the one who had been
desperate for his father's approval. Hated that I had
wasted even a moment seeking it.

"I'm sorry, Michael," Patrick said.

"It was a long time ago," I said, shrugging it off.
"But last night…"

"You know better. I wouldn't do any shit like
that to you. I asked you to make the decision to
show you I trust you," he said.

I instantly believed him, was ashamed I had ever
doubted him.

"Then why?" I asked.

"Why what?" he said.

"Why do you insist that I stay at the hotel?" I said.

"I want to give you options, Michael. And you are too damn hotheaded. But less than you used to be. I've noticed a lot of changes about you, good ones. Despite what Aengus might've told you, a good leader, a strong one, doesn't always have to kill. They use strength and reason. Know when to kill, when to forgive," he said.

"And you think I can do that, even though I killed Arnold?" I said. I'd done what I thought best, but I still wasn't sure Patrick would agree.

"I trust you. You did what you needed to," he said.

"So that's it? You're not going to give me some sappy speech or lecture?"

"I'm your eldest brother. I reserve the right to give you sappy speeches whenever I want. I'll hold it for now, but listen to me and believe me when I tell you Aengus is an asshole. One of the great shames of my life is that I left you and Sean with him, and I only allow him to continue breathing because of that promise we made," he said.

His face had twisted with the rage that Aengus could effortlessly inspire, but Patrick breathed out hard, then looked at me again. He was completely calm and again reminded me why he was the head of our family.

"You're a good person, Michael. An asshole but a good person. I trust you. Now I need you to trust yourself," he said.

———

MICHAEL

Trust myself.

I realized that as simple as that concept seemed, I had so little practice at it. Had none, really.

I'd spent so many years trying to prove that I was worthy of the Murphy name, that I wasn't weak like Aengus had said I was, that I'd lost myself in the process.

No more.

I would prove it, starting now.

I accessed the hotel's personnel records and found Kevin's address. That cheap shot had been a bitch move, and I was brave enough to acknowledge it.

I was also brave enough to not hide. If Eden wanted him, I wouldn't stand in her way. I planned to win her, and I wouldn't make it easy on him, but

I also wouldn't use my name and influence to tilt the field.

It was dark out, but not so late a guest would be completely out of line, so I walked to his door, went to knock. Before I could, I noticed that it was partially open.

My instincts were instantly on alert, and I looked around, saw nothing out of place or out of the ordinary.

At least I didn't until I pushed open the door, my gaze landing on the bloody arm that I could see through the crack.

My phone vibrated, and I looked down at it, my mind racing.

4

A single number. A sign from my brothers that something was wrong.

The last shred of evidence that I was totally fucked.

TWENTY-FIVE

EDEN

When I finally got home, I was in a haze, my mind gone from everything that had happened.

Steve and Bob.

Now Kevin.

I couldn't believe it. I'd just seen him and now he was gone. I thought back to what Gerald had said, wondered if maybe we were cursed.

I dismissed the thought as quickly as it had come. It was stupid, and even more, it opened the door to blaming Michael. I wouldn't even consider that. Everything inside of me left me with no doubt he'd had nothing to do with their deaths.

Perhaps it was a silly thing to think, especially given how little I knew of him. Outside of those few moments when he had shown some hint of vulnerability, those times when he had seemed somewhat protective, there had been nothing to suggest he was anything other than his reputation said. None of that mattered. I knew Michael, and I knew he had nothing to do with this.

I collapsed onto my sofa and flipped on my television, desperate for any distraction.

Distraction, it seemed, that would not be coming.

My eyes were glued to the screen as I watched the news unfold.

I recognized the image instantly because I spent almost all of my waking hours there.

The beautiful architecture that had been hand-selected by the Murphys, that trademark M. I recognized them all, watched in stunned silence as they burned.

The entire structure was engulfed, orange-black flames shooting from the roof.

I was frozen, stunned, almost couldn't believe what I was seeing.

The hotel, the one that I had just left, was burning.

I groped for the remote control and turned the volume up to hear what was said.

"A massive fire has broken out. Authorities told

me that all guests have been safely removed from the hotel, but the building is engulfed. The authorities say it'll be a total loss."

I dropped the remote, ignored it as it clattered silently against the carpet.

The hotel was burning, a total loss.

What a perfect representation of everything that was happening. I almost couldn't believe it but then, I couldn't believe much of what had happened.

I reached for my cell phone, and without taking my eyes off the television, I dialed in the number to the hotel switchboard.

Instead of the expected ring, I got an error message telling me the number was unavailable.

I shouldn't have been surprised and I shouldn't have expected an answer, not when I was watching the hotel light up, seeing the terrified guests and staff gathered outside.

But hearing that message did something, changed something.

Though I had been watching it on television, I hadn't been able to believe what I saw. But calling and not getting an answer proved to me that it was true.

Steve and Bob were dead.

Kevin was dead.

And now the hotel was on fire.

That realization was almost overwhelming and left me feeling shocked, shaky. I hung up, the grating sound of the error message gone. Then I quickly dialed Michael's number. Prayed as fervently as I could that he would answer.

It went directly to voicemail.

I stood, jammed my feet into my shoes, moving in a haze.

I looked at the TV once more, saw the hotel was still on fire. I knew I couldn't stay here, couldn't just wait and watch and do nothing.

I'd go there. Check on the staff, hope that they were all okay.

I grabbed my keys, didn't slow down enough to get my purse, and pulled open my door.

"Oh God!" I screamed when I crashed into a figure.

"Eden. It's me."

I had been on the verge of swinging wildly when I met Gerald's eyes.

"Gerald!"

I acted on instinct, hugged him, my nostrils burning from the acrid smell of smoke on his jacket.

I let go, pulled him into the house.

"Are you okay? What happened?"

He looked over my shoulder toward the television, which still blared. "I see you've heard."

"Yes! I was going there now. What's going on?"

He shook his head. "I think I was right. I think the place is cursed."

"Is everyone okay?" I asked, my mind shifting between disbelief and frantic confusion, confusion that Gerald being here only intensified.

He looked at me, frowned. "Everyone's okay," he replied.

"Come sit! Tell me what happened! We should go back!" I said frantically.

"We should. They are going to need us. Especially after…" he said.

I froze, looked into Gerald's eyes.

"Gerald, are you sure you're okay? You don't seem okay."

I had missed it before, but now I saw that his jacket was ripped, his always tidy clothes looked dirty. Even his thinning gray hair, which was always neatly combed, looked disheveled.

I took a step back, then forced myself to be still.

He looked at me, studying me, his eyes empty,

the blankness in his expression almost scary. Something I had never, ever felt around Gerald.

"You remember before? When we talked about the old times?"

"Yeah…" I said, both impatient and uneasy.

"It can be like that again. But you have to help, Eden," he said.

I was even more wary now, but I took a step closer, lifting my hand, though I didn't reach out to him.

"Gerald," I said slowly, "just tell me what's going on."

He tilted his head. "I tried. But you defended them. Are you going to continue to do that?"

The uneasiness that had been on a low boil notched up to fear.

"Gerald—"

"Eden. Answer. I don't want to do this, but I will," he said.

"Do what?" I asked, my fear notching even higher, my mind screaming that something was very, very wrong.

"Look out the window, Eden," he said.

His voice was flat, completely without inflection, and hearing it made me freeze.

I didn't want to move away from the door, but I

felt compelled, something about his demeanor, his voice making staying still impossible.

I shifted, moved toward my small kitchen, and looked out the window into the backyard.

"Oh my God!"

"So you see. I need your answer, and quickly," he said.

My yard was engulfed, the now-roaring flames, the small wood balcony out back starting to smoke.

"We have to go!" I turned, screamed when I again collided with Gerald.

He held my arms in a tight grip. "Your answer," he said calmly.

"Gerald! You've gone crazy! Let me go!"

I twisted, trying to free myself from him.

"No, that's where you're wrong, Eden. I haven't gone crazy. I've finally seen the way," he said.

"Gerald…what have you done?" I asked, my brain struggling to catch up with what my thudding heart and twisting stomach already knew.

"What I should have done years ago. I realized that I've been playing by the rules. Other people don't."

"Gerald, don't do something you're going to regret," I said, though by looking at him I could tell he wouldn't regret it, didn't want to imagine what he had already done.

"I won't regret it," he said. "At least not all of it."

That last statement filled me with even more dread.

"What does that mean?"

"It means all that I've done, I won't regret it. But what I have to do here...I might..."

"Gerald, you ne—"

I cut off, tried to rush around him.

Almost made it too. But he caught my ankle, and I went tumbling to the ground. I didn't have a chance to brace myself. Instead I landed face-first on the floor. My face burned and my head spun, but I tried to keep moving. When I couldn't, I kicked at Gerald, desperate to get free.

I couldn't.

With strength that surprised me, he pulled me toward him, my shirt ripping as he dragged me along the floor.

"I don't want to do this, Eden," he said, his voice and eyes so calm, it filled me with a soul-shattering dread.

"Answer," he said as he flipped me over.

He trapped me under him, loomed over me, glaring down.

"Gerald, please," I whispered, praying that I could get through to him, terrified that I wouldn't.

"Answer me," he said, his voice almost pleading now.

"Gerald, we can work this out," I said.

"I guess I have my answer," he replied.

Then he closed his hands around my throat.

TWENTY-SIX

MICHAEL

"You see the news?" Declan asked.

I didn't look at him, instead kept my gaze glued to the screen.

"Yeah, I see the news," I said through clenched teeth. I'd heard it on the radio as I'd driven as fast as I dared to Patrick's. Finding a dead body hadn't been ideal, but nothing about this day was shaping up to be.

The TV blared, describing the scene in detail as M. Lounge and Hotel burned to the ground.

"What the fuck is this about, Michael?" Declan asked.

"You think I have any damn idea?" I said, frustrated I had again been caught off guard.

"Then think. There has to be something. That

guy Kevin, those two guards, and now the hotel is on fire. That's not a coincidence," Declan said.

Of course it wasn't a coincidence. But I didn't have any answers.

"Wait," Sean, who was sitting next to me on the sofa, said, "what are you asking?"

Eventually, I'd thank Sean for standing up for me, but for now I could barely do anything, not with the way my mind was racing as I tried to get a handle on what was happening.

"Yeah, Declan," I finally said, "what are you asking?"

I looked at him then, but I don't think he noticed. He and Sean had locked eyes and the silent communication between them was something I could read loud and clear. After a long moment, Declan looked at me.

"Are you asking if I think you killed those men and burned the hotel?" he said.

I appreciated Declan being direct, because that was exactly what I thought, and I told him so.

"Yeah. That's what I think."

"Then you're an idiot. Of course I don't think that. But you obviously got on someone's bad side, and they are working hard to make people think you did. I don't need to remind you that those people are disinclined to give you or the rest of us the benefit of the doubt. So you need to tell me what's going on," he said.

"I..." I trailed off, considering. Not too long ago, I had asked Patrick a similar question. He'd been able to answer quickly if not entirely accurately.

I didn't have that option. Because I couldn't say for sure that no one had it out for me or that I hadn't pissed off the wrong person.

"I don't know," I finally whispered.

I hated confessing that, hated even more that I didn't know, that I couldn't say for sure who might hate me enough to try to frame me.

But when I looked at my brothers, I saw understanding.

"Figure it out," Declan said, his voice stern but his eyes betraying how worried he was.

"Yeah, I will. Where's Patrick?" I asked.

"At the hotel. He wanted to be there, see if they would tell him anything," Declan said.

"Do you think they will?" Sean asked.

Declan shook his head. "No, I don't. He doesn't either, but he wanted to be there anyway."

"I need to be doing something," I said, jumping from the couch and beginning to pace.

"Yeah, you do need to be doing something. And that something is staying put and lying low and letting us handle this. There's no way you can be out there right now, Michael. We don't know what's going on, and with those bodies and the fire, the cops would grab you in a heartbeat."

I knew he was right, but I had a hard time accepting it. Even more, though I wouldn't say it out loud, I was worried about Eden. I couldn't help but wonder what she was thinking of me, if she thought the worst of me as I suspected everyone else did.

I hoped she didn't, but I realized now I hadn't given her reason not to. I'd never opened myself to her fully, never given her any real hint of what I felt. She had every reason to believe the worst.

I didn't know if I'd ever have a chance to prove to her otherwise.

Declan slid his arms into his leather jacket and I watched him curiously. "Where are you going?"

"That's unimportant. What's important is that you stay put. Sean, you stay here with him and babysit," Declan said.

"I guess I can handle that," Sean replied.

Declan looked between us, his expression serious. "I mean it. Both of you stay put. Don't make this worse."

After another moment's pause, he left.

Less than ten seconds passed before I looked at Sean. He met my eyes, a little smile on his face.

"I'll drive," he said.

———

MICHAEL

"So where are we going?" Sean asked.

"You didn't ask that before we left," I said.

"No, because it didn't matter. I'm with you no matter where we go. So where are we going?" he said, glancing at me before he looked back at the road.

"Eden's house," I said.

I felt some residual embarrassment at admitting that to Sean, but he simply nodded, then turned the car in that direction. I was relieved because I would see her soon, and once I knew she was safe, I'd be able to focus on what the hell was happening.

"You know where she lives?" I asked Sean a moment later.

"Yep," he said without adding more.

Just twenty-four hours ago, I would have been

furious at him for that, but now I didn't care. Those brief hours had left me no question as to what was important, and nothing, not even a chance to snipe at Sean, was more important than getting to her.

As Sean turned the car down Eden's quiet street, I focused on her house.

My brain fought to deny what my eyes saw, but the black smoke that billowed from her roof, the way Sean sped the vehicle couldn't be denied.

"Michael, wait—"

I didn't hear what else Sean had to say, because before the car had fully come to a stop, I jumped out and ran toward the house.

The door stood wide open and a body lay on her front steps. Seeing it told me I had been right to come here and made me wonder if I was too late.

I only looked at the prone form long enough to confirm that it wasn't Eden, and once I had, I rushed inside.

The heat, the thick, billowing black smoke was overwhelming, but not as explosive as the worry that made my heart boom.

"Eden!"

I called for her, looked around wildly, ignoring the way my lungs burned, the way my eyes stung from the smoke.

None of that mattered, because I had to find her.

Would find her.

I made my way through the living room as best I could, knocking down anything in my path. I cursed myself for not knowing her home better, for not taking the time to.

"Eden!"

I yelled as loud as I could, my voice frantic, but not nearly as frantic as I felt inside.

I had to find her, wouldn't let her die like this, and I promised myself that whoever had done this would suffer, suffer so very mightily.

"Eden!" I screamed again.

Then I stood still, listening, hoping for some sound that would lead me toward her. I could barely hear anything over my pounding heart, but after a second, I heard something. I might have been imagining it, but I thought I heard a cough.

Hope, relief, unlike any I had ever felt lifted me, and I moved toward that sound, desperate to find her.

When I saw her lying there, her hair unruly, her face covered with soot, I rushed to her.

"Eden!" I yelled, a sound that was cut off when smoke began to fill my lungs.

Still, I tried to keep focused, held her to me, my heart dropping when I saw the blood that dripped along her hairline, fear that she was gone threatening.

Then she moved and I was able to breathe again.

As gingerly as I could, I lifted her and then carried her out, tried not to jar her while still moving as fast as I possibly could.

When I went through the front door again and took my first deep breath, I thought my chest would explode from the relief.

Relief that was short-lived.

I gingerly laid Eden on the ground, then held her face, moved down her neck to find her pulse.

It was strong, and she was coughing.

I willed her to move.

She didn't.

My heart was beating so fast, I was light-headed, but I was completely focused on Eden.

"You can wake up now," I whispered, brushing my hand over her hair.

She didn't move, and her stillness, the horrible thought of what that meant crushed me.

"Eden," I said, practically yelling, "wake up. Now." I used the voice I knew she hated, hoped that it would piss her off enough to wake up and tell me to shove it.

She didn't move.

"Michael, Gerald's over there," Sean whispered.

I'd forgotten about the person who'd been lying on her front steps when I'd arrived, but when Sean pointed at him, I turned, saw him on the ground.

"Gerald, what are you doing here?" I asked forcefully.

He rolled, brought himself to his knees, his suit jacket still buttoned though it was ripped, blackened with ash.

He looked at me, and when I looked into his eyes, I saw a glimmer of pure malice. Then, right before my eyes, he morphed, his face breaking, tears springing from his eyes.

"Oh God! He tried to kill her! Tried to kill me!" Gerald screamed.

I tightened my grip on Eden but kept my eyes on him, my stomach dropping as I watched him, everything in me certain this horrible day was going to get worse.

Gerald fell on his backside and then began to crawl away from me, moving away from the house and me with wide eyes, his hand extended, finger pointing at me in accusation.

"It was him!"

In an instant, I knew. Gerald was behind this. He hated me so much, he'd hurt Eden to get to me. At that moment, I'd never wanted to kill anyone as much as I did Gerald, not even my father.

I might not have the chance.

"What the fuck are you talking about, asshole?" Sean said.

At the sound of his voice, Gerald looked over, screamed, and then began to crawl faster.

"Help! Help!" he cried.

I wanted to go after him but couldn't leave Eden's side. So instead, I held her hand, waited.

"Sean, get an ambulance," I said. I'd deal with Gerald. Eden was what mattered now.

"On its way," he responded, though he didn't take his eyes off Gerald, who had now crawled toward the street screaming.

"He tried to kill me!"

"If you want to get out of here, now's the time," he said.

I looked at him, then looked down at Eden, knowing there was no way I would leave her side.

"I'm not going anywhere," I said, wrapping my hand around hers.

TWENTY-SEVEN

EDEN

"Michael!"

That was the first word that came out of my mouth after my eyes flew open.

I looked around wildly, saw I was in a hospital room. Touched my face and felt the plastic oxygen tubes that were in my nose, looked down and saw the IV in my arm.

Scanned the room again and saw that Michael was nowhere to be found.

My chest burned, my head throbbed, but I remembered what had happened, knew that the hotel and my home were gone.

And Michael wasn't here.

I'd thought I was going to die in that house, had

tried so hard to find my way out but hadn't been able to muster the strength.

But when I'd looked up, seen him through the plumes of smoke coming toward me like an angel sent to rescue me, I had known I would be okay.

Now he was gone.

"You okay?"

I glanced over at the sound of the male voice, saw that it was Sean.

"What are you doing here?" I asked, sounding defensive, confused, something I was entitled to.

"Top of the morning, Eden," he said, giving me his usual smile, his green eyes not quite as bright as they normally were.

"Where is he?" I asked.

My throat was raw, my voice hoarse, but I didn't care about that. Didn't care about anything but Michael.

"He's been arrested," Sean said.

"Arrested? For what?" I asked, gaping at him.

"Three counts of murder. Two counts of attempted murder. Two counts of arson," Sean said.

His voice had no inflection, but I could see the tightness in his face, in the way he held his body.

"Oh my God!" I exclaimed, the pieces falling into place instantly. "They can't do that! Gerald is behind this. He set it all up to get back at Michael."

"Yeah, but the cops don't care. They think they have him, and they aren't going to let this chance pass," Sean said.

He looked as angry as I felt. But even more than angry, I felt powerless and to blame. I'd ignored the tension for years, pretended Gerald would get over it, and in doing so, I had put myself in danger, and now Michael was paying the price.

"Don't look like that, Eden. We'll fix this," Sean said firmly.

I didn't believe it.

"This isn't about me or Kevin or the guards. It's not really about Michael at all either, is it?" I asked, my stomach dropping, knots pulling it tight.

"No," Sean said, his expression pulled down, his face now as emotionless as I'd ever seen it.

"But Patrick's going to fix it…" I let the question dangle, not wanting to consider the possibility that Patrick couldn't, knowing it was a possibility all the same.

"We're on it," Sean said, an attempt to comfort me, one that didn't help at all. Then he flashed me a small smile. The expression was one unlike I had seen from him, equally sad and determined. "But you need to rest, get well. Michael will be pissed if I don't take care of you."

I nodded, then looked out the window. Sean wanted me to rest, but I couldn't do that, not without Michael.

———

MICHAEL

Surprisingly, I was unfamiliar with the inside of a police interrogation room.

Declan wasn't, Sean sure as hell wasn't, and though Patrick had been indicted, neither he nor I had ever been formally arrested.

I looked around the small room, tested the cuffs that joined my wrists.

Guessed this was something I could check off the list.

Everything about this, from the small, suffocating hot room, to the cuffs that had been pulled tighter than they needed to be, was designed to break me, or at least make me uncomfortable.

It wouldn't work.

I could see the manipulation from a mile away, was resolved not to be taken in by it. Still, I was anxious, antsy, and not because of my surroundings.

When Gerald had put on his little show, I hadn't had any doubt that the police would believe him. However, the ruse wouldn't hold, and until then, I'd keep it together.

But as the hours had ticked by, my worry was increasing.

Eden was alive.

She was, and I wouldn't consider anything else, but I didn't know her condition.

As they'd pushed me into the police car, I called at Sean to stay with Eden, and I was certain that he would. I needed to see her myself, make sure she was okay.

Tell her how I felt.

I didn't know that it would matter.

She probably believed the worst of me, something I was sure that asshole Gerald had made sure of. Even if she did believe me, she wouldn't want to have anything to do with me after the danger I'd put her in.

But I couldn't control that, couldn't see her, couldn't make this all right, not when I was locked in this room.

I was sure they were watching me, waiting for an opening. I wouldn't give it to them.

There had been a time when I was so certain of

my own self-control, but that time had passed. I would hold it together, and then I would see Eden.

Nothing else mattered.

I reminded myself of that as the seconds ticked by, the tight walls of the room robbing me of any sense of time. I didn't know how much later it was when the door opened.

A detective walked in, glaring at me through the open door.

"You have a visitor," he said.

I didn't respond, but I was curious.

When Gerald walked through the door, I clenched my cuffed hands, fought to keep the scowl off my face as that curiosity shifted to venomous rage.

He looked triumphant, at least when I was watching him. When the detective looked at him, he shrank back into his reserved, formal shell, looking battered and broken.

If I hadn't known any better, I would have seen the image of an older professional man who was cowering in fear of a monster.

Patrick should have listened when I told him to fire this jerk-off. When I got out of this, I'd make sure he never lived it down.

If I got out of it.

Gerald looked at me, his eyes watery, his hands clenched tight at his chest. Then, after a dramatic pause that made me want to puke and roll my eyes, he looked at the detective, nodded.

"Yes, it's him," he said breathlessly.

"What are you doing here?" I said, keeping my voice as calm, even, as I possibly could.

"He's making an official identification," the detective interjected, a triumphant note in his voice.

"Isn't there protocol for that?" I asked blandly, knowing he was trying to get under my skin. I wouldn't let him.

"I ask the questions, asshole, not you," the detective said.

I ignored him and turned my gaze back to Gerald. I hoped my face didn't betray what I was thinking. I had plans for Gerald. He'd spend the rest of his short life in excruciating pain, and he'd only live long enough to regret what he'd done to Eden.

Gerald knew that. I could see that from the little flash of fear in his eyes.

It went away quickly, but it was there.

I wondered if Gerald had thought this through. I might not ever get out of this room, but even if that happened, it wouldn't change anything for him.

"I'm just so…" Gerald broke my gaze and then looked at the detective, who patted his shoulder sympathetically.

"I know this is rough, Gerald, but once you do this, *he* won't be able to hurt you or Eden or anyone else ever again," the detective said.

The detective was very wrong about that, but I kept myself expressionless as Gerald blanched at the mention of Eden. At least momentarily, some of my rage banked, relief leaving me flushed.

Eden had made it, something Gerald hadn't counted on. I wanted to rub his face in that, tell him in excruciating detail what I was going to do to him, but I kept my mouth closed.

I could see the wheels turning in Gerald's head, narrowed my eyes when his shoulders slumped.

"What?" the detective asked.

"Eden… She's such a lovely girl. So confused," Gerald said. He spoke like a sympathetic, sorrowful friend, and something in his words put me on alert.

The detective looked at him, interested now, so interested, he seemed to forget about my presence.

"What do you mean by that, Mr. Collins?"

"I'm afraid that Eden is under his influence.

They had a relationship of a…sexual nature. I'm afraid it's influenced her," Gerald said regretfully.

That fucker had tried to kill her and now he was selling her out. I hadn't thought it possible, but my hatred for Gerald increased.

"I wasn't aware of that," the detective replied, looking at me with even more scorn.

"I wasn't either until recently. Maybe my discovery was what pushed him over the edge and made him do all those terrible things."

I held my tongue, but from the way Gerald shrank back, I knew my expression gave more than a clue to my thoughts. With great effort, I wiped all expression from my face, kept my eyes on Gerald. I wouldn't give them any ammunition.

Gerald shook his head, looking regretful. "It's a shame. All those years of friendship led me to believe I knew Eden. I guess keeping company with someone like him can change you."

When Gerald looked at me again, his eyes again flashed with triumph. He thought he'd won, and from this seat, I was in no position to argue.

The detective opened the door and led Gerald out. I tested the cuffs again, again found them unyielding, and realized I was more powerless than

I'd ever been before. It had never mattered more than it did now.

TWENTY-EIGHT

EDEN

"You want some real food?" Sean asked.

"No," I responded, trying and failing to keep the listlessness out of my voice.

"What about a diet soda? I seem to recall you love that shit," he said.

I snorted and then smiled at Sean appreciatively. "Yeah, that would be nice," I said.

"Be back. Don't go anywhere," he replied.

I wouldn't, mostly because my head would crack in two if I tried, and because Sean was the one connection, however tenuous it was, to Michael, so I wouldn't leave his side until I knew Michael was okay.

Until I had a chance to explain to him what had happened.

I'd told Sean the story, had no doubt he would tell Patrick, get a message to Michael, but that wasn't good enough.

I wanted to speak the words.

And I wanted to apologize.

If I'd said something sooner, done more, maybe Gerald wouldn't have snapped. Even if he had, maybe Michael would have been able to prepare. But I'd said nothing, and now Michael was suffering.

Then I thought back to being in my burning home, fearing I might die before I had a chance to tell him how I felt.

But I wasn't dead—I still had that chance.

"Are you well, dear?"

I froze at the sound of Gerald's voice, looked at him, shocked that he had the balls to make an appearance. It spoke poorly of me that Gerald still had the ability to shock me. The man had bashed in his own head, set a house that he was inside of on fire.

Nothing was beyond him.

I studied him, looked at the lumpy purplish bruise on his head, the fresh suit he wore, wondered how I had missed the insanity in his eyes.

"You have a question," he said, looking at me knowingly.

"What the fuck happened to you, Gerald?" I said.

He smiled, shook his head. "Such language. Ah, the company you keep. But to answer your question, not that you deserve one, the Murphys happened to me. As I explained before, they took all that mattered to me. Do you think they'd have shouldered the burden so well had the roles been reversed?" he said.

"You have no idea what a burden is, Gerald," Sean said, reentering the room.

I looked toward the door, saw that Sean looked angry, something I couldn't ever really recall him being.

Gerald just smiled, an expression that chilled my blood.

"Are you insinuating I should be concerned for my safety, Mr. Murphy?"

Sean squeezed the can in his hand, curled his free hand into a fist, but he didn't speak. Gerald had the upper hand here, something he knew, I knew, and Sean knew.

"Quiet," Gerald said, a smile curling his lips. "Such a change for you and a welcome one. Don't worry, I think I'm going to sleep just fine. If I get so much as a hangnail, who do you think they will hold responsible? Now that the authorities are questioning Eden's relationship with your brother, her word won't help you either."

"Get the fuck out," Sean growled.

"Gladly. Now that I've seen that Eden is okay, I can get on with things."

Gerald turned and left then, and Sean stood for a moment, staring after him, his rigid stance telling me exactly what he thought.

Then he turned and began to approach me, holding the soda out toward me.

"I don't think this is your brand," he said.

Before I answered, I popped the can open and took that first refreshing sip. Then, after I had caught my breath, calmed my nerves as much as I possibly could, I looked at him.

"No, it's not," I whispered. "But thank you."

He nodded, then sat down. The air in the room felt heavy, and when I looked at Sean, I could see that his expression mirrored my own concern, his eyes looking weighted behind his glasses.

After a moment, he tilted his head, his green eyes twinkling, a little smile playing on his face.

"I told you that guy was an asshole," he said.

For the first time in hours, I smiled.

———

MICHAEL

"Wake up," a gruff, unfriendly voice called.

I hadn't been sleeping, but rather than correcting the guard, I simply stood.

The others in the holding cell looked at me curiously, but no one said anything. It had been the same for days, me keeping to myself, the others unwilling to approach me. Which was good, because I was nearing the end of my rope, and a fight was just the thing I needed if getting out of here wasn't an option.

That wouldn't have been smart. They were looking for any excuse to keep me, and fortunately, none of the other prisoners had given me a reason to give them one.

"Sign here. Sign here. Here's your shit," the female guard sitting at the processing desk said as she shoved a manila envelope into my hands.

I signed, took the envelope and opened it. My belongings smelled charred, instantly reminded me of that fire, of Eden, but I kept my face passive and walked out to the waiting SUV.

I got inside and saw that Declan was driving and Patrick was in the front seat.

"You okay?" Patrick asked, meeting my eyes through the rearview.

"I'm good," I said. "Now, take me to Eden."

"You're welcome," Declan said gruffly.

"Take me to Eden," I responded.

"Michael, that's not an option," Patrick said. "You have to lie low right now."

I was close to my breaking point, beginning to fray, but when I looked at him, saw the concern in his eyes, I knew something was wrong. I was instantly on edge, my mind leaping to Eden and her safety.

"She'd better be okay," I said.

"Eden's fine," Declan said. "Sean is with her."

"So what's the problem?" I asked, looking from Declan to Patrick and back again.

It was Declan who finally spoke.

"The problem is Gerald Collins is dead. And you're the number one suspect in his murder."

TWENTY-NINE

EDEN

"You'll be fine here, so just relax," Sean said.

It had been a day since I got out of the hospital, and now that I was at Patrick's house, the unbearable tension and worry of before had only intensified.

I hadn't seen Michael, and other than telling me that he was out of jail, no one had given me any updates.

I did know Gerald was dead.

Too much had happened in these last days for me to be shocked, but I was worried.

The police had questioned me about his murder. Fortunately, my stay at the hospital had proven a convenient alibi. I'd thought that Michael being in jail would be an alibi for him, but Sean had gently explained that Michael wouldn't have to do commit the act personally to be responsible.

Between the Murphys and their very high-priced lawyers, I hadn't had to deal with the police again, but when they'd questioned me, they'd asked questions about Gerald but had quickly moved to questions about Michael, their desire to have me implicate him, perhaps all of the Murphys, clear.

Something I would never do.

I hadn't even bothered to ask if Michael or the others had been involved. Gerald had been right that killing him would be stupid, and Michael wasn't that.

Sean had explained that Michael and I needed to stay apart for now, and though I understood, I didn't like it, hated it in fact. And Patrick's generosity, his lovely home, didn't come close to filling the emptiness that came from missing Michael.

I was sitting in the kitchen, a bright, airy room, and I turned when the French doors that led to the lovely grounds opened.

"Would you like to come sit outside with us?" Nya, Patrick's wife asked.

She looked at me kindly, with compassion, as she had since the day I had arrived. The shorter woman next to her was openly assessing me, her gaze not hostile, but certainly skeptical.

Before I could answer Nya's question, she spoke. "You're the assistant GM of the hotel, right?"

"Yeah." I shrugged. "At least I used to be."

She sighed. "Remind me never to stay there. Not that I even have the option anymore."

I frowned at her and Nya did too before she looked at me apologetically.

"Don't mind my dear friend Jade. She was just leaving and she had no home training," Nya said.

Jade snorted. "None at all. Take care of yourself, girl," she said, hugging Nya and then giving me a little wave before she left.

I couldn't help but laugh in her wake, something I'd done far too little of recently. Nya did the same and then sat beside me on one of the kitchen bar stools.

"Sorry for intruding," I said.

She shook her head and smiled at me kindly. "It's no intrusion. You're welcome here for as long as you need to be, and I'm happy to lend an ear if you need it," she said.

"I appreciate it," I replied.

We went quiet for a moment and then she

looked at me, studying me. "This is a tough situation, but try not to worry too much."

"You sound pretty certain that I shouldn't be worried," I said.

She smiled. "I am."

I returned the smile, but my mind spun with fear. "I hope you're right, Nya," I whispered.

————

MICHAEL

"I have a son named Michael," my mother said, her eyes bright, her face smiling, carefree.

"I know. I've met him," I replied.

"Good. He's a nice boy," she said.

Then she was gone, lost in whatever world she was trapped in. For the first time, it occurred to me she might be exactly where she wanted to be.

I wasn't sure why I had come here, but I had felt compelled, and was now glad I had. She wasn't herself, hadn't been in decades, but seeing her still comforted me.

Right now, I needed all the comfort I could get.

We were no closer to figuring out who had killed Gerald and until we did, Patrick and Patrick's lawyers, who he paid a fucking fortune, insisted I not see Eden.

I hated it, would have insisted otherwise, but when I was reminded people could, and would, use her to get to me and my brothers, I didn't fight.

I had done enough to destroy her life. I wouldn't do more.

"I'll see you later, Maura," I called.

"Okay. Maybe you can bring my Michael next time," she said.

"Maybe," I replied.

I made my way toward the exit, the one that I had paid extra to use so that I couldn't be seen, turned the corner.

Found Aengus there.

My anger was instant.

"I thought I told you not to come here anymore," I said.

"You told me not to see her," he said, pointing at me. "I'm here to see you."

He had said that to get a reaction, something I was intent on not giving him.

"What do you want from me?"

"I heard you were having some trouble. Thought I'd check on you," he said.

"Yeah right, Aengus," I said.

He shook his head, tsked at me. "You've been under your brothers' thumbs for too long. They've influenced you, turned you against me."

"You did that yourself," I said.

"What?" Aengus said, feigning ignorance.

I didn't buy it.

He knew exactly what I was talking about, and I held his gaze, unwilling to look away. He waved a dismissive hand.

"You still hung up on that shit from when you were a kid?"

I said nothing but Aengus waved again, the shit he'd done to me mattering no more now than it ever had.

"Fuck off," I said, moving to go past him.

He put a hand on my shoulder and I glared at him until he dropped it.

"Fine. But for what it's worth, I was thinking about going to the cops. Telling them there's no way you were involved in that asshole's murder," Aengus said.

I frowned, wondering what his angle was.

"You'd speak on my behalf?" I asked.

He frowned. "I wouldn't call it that, but they are misinformed. If they knew anything at all, they'd know the weakest of my sons is too much of a pussy to hurt a fly. At this point, I doubt his brothers would either."

To my surprise, Aengus's insult rolled off me completely. I was too distracted with trying to figure out what he was up to. As I tried to read his expression, I saw his near glee. Felt like the truth hit me like a ton of bricks.

"You motherfucker!" I said.

His eyes twinkled, and he tilted his head, shrugged. "Maybe you have some friends who care about your well-being."

I expected nothing from Aengus, knew what he was capable of. But this…

"What do you hope to gain from this, Aengus?"

"Gain? I just want the world to know that not everyone in my fucking family will take shit lying down," he said.

After one last taunting smile, he turned and left.

This was so fucked, but I kind of admired Aengus and his crude but effective genius.

He'd killed Gerald, and in the process projected an air of protecting his name while planting the seeds of my destruction. Aengus had cost me my childhood, and now he'd put my only chance at happiness at risk.

I walked back to the SUV in a haze, and when I

got in, I barely looked at Sean before I said, "Take me to Eden."

Sean drove off without protest.

THIRTY

EDEN

I'd spent another day wandering aimlessly through Patrick's house, chatting with Nya. Wondering what had become of my life.

But mostly thinking about Michael.

Everything had changed so much that I didn't know where to begin, didn't know how to reconcile what it had been just days ago with the new reality I faced.

Because I had lost everything.

My home.

My job.

Had almost been killed by a man I'd counted among my closest friends.

But all that seemed distant, almost meaningless in Michael's absence.

Which was insane.

If anything, I should blame him for my current predicament, should consider his role in all that had happened. I didn't, I didn't think of anything but how much I wanted to see him.

Suddenly, he was there.

I'd decided to hide out in the guest room, feeling much like an intruder even though Nya had ensured me I wasn't. I was staring out the window at the beautiful yard, hoping I would see something or at the very least that the view would give me some comfort.

"You look really comfortable in my house."

At the sound of Michael's voice, I turned, halfway convinced I had simply imagined it.

When my eyes collided with his, I knew he was real, knew I was finally seeing him again.

I stood, rushed to him, uncaring of anything except touching him.

I'd played this moment out a thousand times in my head, knew I would be relieved, but insisted I would keep my cool, not show just how much I'd missed him.

All of that flew right out of the window when I saw him.

I moved without pause, throwing my arms around him and squeezing him close.

It was only when he squeezed me back that I realized what I had done. I shifted in his arms and looked up at him, gauging his reaction.

Maybe he would find that display of affection off-putting, unnecessary.

Irritating, like he so often did me.

I didn't know, but when I looked at him, saw his somewhat dour expression, but the relief in his eyes, I felt an almost immediate sense of happiness.

In a flash, the air between us became different, heated, and I leaned close to him, tilted my head to meet his lips as he kissed me.

The caress was soft, gentle, probing, and I could hear the unspoken question in it, the same one I had seen in his eyes.

"I'm fine," I whispered against his mouth.

I opened my eyes and met his, saw that he was searching, probing for truth, his eyes and expression going stony as he traced the scratches and bruises that remained with his fingertips.

My eyes welled as Michael touched me, the care in his touch so much more than words, the tentativeness in it telling me he wasn't so sure.

"I'm okay, Michael," I whispered.

He kissed me again, this time harsher, stronger, reminding me of the Michael who had almost instantly won me over. I reveled in that kiss, loving the feeling of his hands touching me, the way he guided me backward.

He tugged at the shirt I wore, one I had gotten from Nya. It was ill-fitting, loose in some places, tighter in others, and far too long since she was so much taller than me.

Michael didn't seem to care, and I certainly didn't, cared even less when he tossed the garment aside and cupped my breasts, kneading them in his hands as he kissed me.

Instantly, my blood heated, the need and desire for him, the absolute relief at seeing him again leaving me light-headed. But not so much that I didn't kiss him back, pour every ounce of emotion I could muster into it.

Words had left me, and I didn't know if I had any that could convey how much I missed him, how much I loved him. Maybe I couldn't say it with words, but I would show him as best I could.

I moved my hand down, curled my fingers around his heavy hardness, wanting to deepen our connection.

He broke the kiss, his breath coming out in my own.

He looked down at me, watching with approval as I pulled open the buttons of his shirt, slid it down his shoulders, my mind going back to that first night at my house.

Unlike that night, Michael wasn't patient, slow. When his shirt was gone, he moved fast, removing the rest of his clothes and mine as he kissed me, almost in a frenzy. A frenzy I understood.

I kissed Michael back as hard and fast as he kissed me, tried to touch all of him at once.

And when he entered me, I knew I would never let him go.

———

MICHAEL

"What happened?"

Eden's question was a soft whisper, one that she followed with a gentle caress of my face.

I didn't respond immediately, and instead held her a little bit tighter, allowing myself to steal the comfort that being with her brought, not knowing when, if, I would have the chance to do so again.

I cursed myself for my stupidity, the way I had deprived myself of this.

Eden's body, the physical pleasure I found with her was unrivaled, but this, the comfort, the joy of simply being with her was something I had been too stupid, too stubborn to allow myself.

I might live to regret that.

"Michael…"

At the sound of her voice, I opened my eyes, lifted my head.

"There's another warrant out for my arrest," I said.

She looked at me, frowned.

"Gerald?" she asked.

I nodded.

"But Patrick, your lawyers…"

"Are going to do what they can, but Gerald was a witness. The judge isn't likely to let me go, not with the other counts," I said, not allowing any emotion to fill my voice.

"But they can't…" She trailed off, met my eyes again. "I'll try again. I've been trying to tell everyone that Gerald was behind it," she said, her voice edging toward frantic.

"I appreciate it, but it won't help," I said, letting

my face lift into a grin. "You can't be trusted, not with the kind of company you keep."

Eden didn't look amused, and instead her brows dipped further, her expression one of anger.

"They can't just railroad you because of your name!" she said.

"It's more than a name, Eden," I said, my voice taking on an edge that hadn't been there before. I'd never had this conversation with anyone, and I didn't know how Eden would react. What I and my family did was no secret, but it wasn't something that I ever discussed with outsiders.

Not that Eden was an outsider, not anymore.

I didn't know whether it was intentional, but she dropped her gaze to my arm, her eyes lingering on the M. I had tattooed there, an emblem I wore proudly and always would.

"Are you saying you killed Gerald?" she asked, articulating the words with a degree of care that made me wonder if Eden believed I had, whether that belief would be the end of us.

"No," I responded, studying her expression for any hint of her reaction. She didn't outright object, but I didn't know if she completely believed me, either, and I didn't want to press the issue.

"But I don't know if it matters," I finished.

She looked at me, shaking her head. "No. No, Michael," she said.

"'No' what?"

"You're not going to do that. You're not going to give up. You're going to fight with every breath. You will *not* give up. I won't let you," she said so fiercely, I couldn't do anything but believe her.

I was stunned with the ferocity of her reaction, but even more by what it meant. I'd worried that maybe some of what Gerald had said had gotten to her. Thought that if it hadn't, his attack and the destruction of her house would have turned her against me.

It hadn't, and she hadn't. No, she was expressing a belief in me that no one but my brothers ever had.

If I didn't already love her, I would've lost my heart to her completely.

"I'm not going to give up. I just want you to understand," I said.

"I don't," she said, frowning. "I don't understand, and I won't. This can't stand, Michael, I'm going to…"

"You're going to stay here and do exactly what Patrick tells you," I said firmly.

"So I'm just supposed to sit here while they try to pin this on you?"

"You don't understand what you're dealing with here, Eden. I can take care of myself, but I can't do that if I'm worried…"

I trailed off, that natural instinct not to admit the truth, the urge not to show any kind of weakness momentarily taking over. But I pushed that to the side, knew that if ever there was a time to show what I felt, it was now. "I just need to know you're here and you're safe."

She frowned. "You think I'm in danger? Gerald's dead."

"He is, but I just need to know," I said, not telling her about Aengus, not even knowing how to begin that conversation. Besides, it didn't really matter.

What mattered was that she was okay and that I would be able to take care of her.

"Promise me," I said, staring into her eyes.

She was still for a moment and then curled her lips into a smile.

"You know, I wouldn't ordinarily accept you being pushy with me, Mr. Murphy," she said. She smiled a little brighter, though there was lingering sadness in her eyes. "But just this once I'll make an exception."

―――――

MICHAEL

One Week Later

The chains around my ankles slowed my gait, but not too much.

I walked into the courtroom with as much pride as I could muster, the suit Patrick had seen that I received not doing much to detract from the fact I was in chains.

Today was my first hearing, and the lawyer had warned me not to expect a favorable outcome. An unnecessary admonition, because I'd learned long ago never to do such a thing.

That hadn't really mattered before. Good, bad, indifferent, I'd always known I would be okay, but this was different. Because my freedom was on the line, as was the one chance to be happy with the woman I loved more than life itself.

When I saw my brothers in the front row, Eden sandwiched between Sean and Patrick, my heart simultaneously jumped and dropped.

I didn't show it though and instead walked to the defendant's table, anxious to see how the day would unfold, holding to the tiny shred of hope I would be able to get back to Eden.

The prosecutor, one who I knew was excited about the prospect of taking down one of the Murphys, presented her argument, one that was damned compelling even if it was utter bullshit.

"It's more than a coincidence that the key witness in three homicides against the defendant has turned up dead. A defendant with known ties to organized crime. You can't risk allowing this criminal onto the streets, Your Honor," she said, finishing with a flourish.

My lawyer stood and said, "Your Honor, Mr. Murphy is an upstanding citizen and business owner. Before this witch hunt, he'd never even been arrested."

He continued, putting up a valiant argument, and I knew exactly where this was going.

Nowhere.

The judge studied me, each second that passed confirming what I expected.

"These are serious charges," she said, speaking to my lawyer but looking at me.

"Of course they are, and my client is eager to prove his innocence. He shouldn't be deprived of his freedom while he waits for his chance," my lawyer said.

The judge went quiet, studying me.

The atmosphere in the room was thick, near silent, and I could see my chance slipping away.

The urge to look for Eden, try to find some comfort was strong, but I wouldn't give in to it. There was no shame in it, but I needed to keep focused, keep my mind on this. I didn't know if I would be able to do that if I looked at her and had to confront the idea of losing her after I'd only just found her.

"Your Honor?"

The sound of the timid, whispered words wouldn't have been audible on an ordinary day, but in the courtroom, one that was so heavy and dense with silence, it rang out.

The judge, who had looked down and begun flipping through papers, lifted her eyes to the gallery in search of the sound. I followed her gaze, landed on a man I recognized. He was a maintenance man at the hotel.

"Quiet," the bailiff barked.

"I'm sorry. I just…"

"You're interrupting my court proceedings," the judge said, her icy stare seeming to make the man shrivel.

He swallowed, his throat moving, but he didn't sit. "I'm sorry, but I tried to call the prosecutor. No one will talk to me, so this is my only choice."

The judge looked annoyed, but said, "What's so important that you're disrupting these proceedings?"

"Mr. Murphy didn't do it," the man said.

I studied the man as my heart leapt. He was coming to my defense, but I was skeptical and wouldn't allow myself hope.

The audible gasp in the courtroom was followed by the prosecutor jumping to her feet. "Your Honor, this is highly irregular, and I ask that you put a stop to it."

"How do you know that?" the judge said, ignoring the prosecutor.

"I—I saw someone. It wasn't him," he said. The man sounded certain, and I couldn't help but wonder if Aengus had been that sloppy or if this was a part of his scheme.

Despite myself, hope started to grow in my chest, though I tried to squash it. This wasn't a sure thing and I couldn't forget that.

"Your Honor, I think it's outrageous that one of this man's hired goons is disrupting your courtroom and making a charade of this process. Put an end to it!" the prosecutor yelled.

"This court is in recess," the judge called, slamming her gavel on the bench.

I looked at my lawyer—he looked back at me, his expression unmoving. I couldn't read him at all, and that meant no one else could either. My first impression of the guy was that he was a slick asshole, but if he managed to help get me out of here, he'd be worth every penny.

He lifted a notepad and held it in front of his face and then leaned in close to me to whisper. "Are you behind this?" he asked, his voice steely.

I met his eyes, then shook my head a fraction of an inch.

He held my gaze and then finally let out a little smile.

"Then today is your lucky day."

THIRTY-ONE

MICHAEL

My lawyer had been right.

It had taken hours, but the judge had listened to the maintenance man's story, looked at the rest of the evidence, and, after my lawyer made a motion, dismissed the indictment.

His word alone hadn't been enough to sway her, but taken together with some other interesting evidence we had uncovered about Gerald, including the fact that he had purchased a large amount of the same type of accelerant that was used to burn down M. Hotel and Lounge, she'd been convinced.

The prosecutor had been furious, and I wouldn't have been surprised if those charges came back, but at least for today, I was free. I took what felt like my first breath in days, and my heart soared as I thought of this chance to be with Eden.

Patrick had taken her away earlier, and as I left the courtroom, I saw the maintenance man standing outside the building.

I walked toward him, assessing, trying to figure out if he had an angle.

"Why did you do that?" I asked.

He froze, probably at my tone, then twisted his hands.

"It's the truth," he said.

"That's not an answer," I replied.

He looked at me, studying me now, before he finally spoke.

"Do you remember Trudy?" he asked.

I thought back until I identified the person who belonged to that name. "The old lady in housekeeping?"

When I had first taken over the hotel, the ancient woman had been the head of the housekeeping department. It took her the entire day to finish one room, and in addition to being inefficient as hell, an old lady doing that kind of labor was something I hadn't liked.

"Yeah," the man said. "By the time you came in, she wasn't fit to do much more than fold towels."

"And?" I asked, trying not to be impatient, but not clear why any of that mattered.

"And you kept her on. Let her come in every day even though she wasn't doing anything."

"That was Eden's idea," I said.

"Yeah. But you remember that new equipment we got? Made work so much easier. And then those health plans. More than a handful of us were finally able to get our kids braces," he said.

"That was also Eden's idea. Nothing that would compel you to help me. It's not like I was particularly nice to any of you," I said.

The man chuckled, his face lit with amusement before he sobered.

"That's true, but nice doesn't pay the bills. Eden is a lovely woman, so it might have been her ideas, but it was your money. You were decent to us, something most folks aren't," he said.

I looked at him, disbelieving. "So you came to open court, risked contempt because of a dental plan?" I asked incredulously, not quite believing it.

He shrugged. "You reap what you sow, right?"

I was still thinking about what the man had said when I got into the waiting SUV.

"You ready to go to Patrick's?" Sean asked.

"I need to make a stop first," I said.

We arrived at my mother's facility a little more than half an hour later.

Sean stayed in the car, something that didn't surprise me at all, as I made my way to the side entrance.

We were at her facility, but I wasn't coming to see her. About fifteen minutes after I arrived, Aengus emerged from the entrance, just as I had expected him to.

"I guess it's no coincidence that you're here, right?" I asked.

Aengus grinned. "The minute you get your freedom, you run directly to your mommy. Can't say I'm surprised," he said.

"That's where you're mistaken, Aengus. I came here to see you," I said.

He looked surprised. "Am I hallucinating? One of my ungrateful little bastards is thanking me?" he said.

"No," I said, "I didn't come to thank you. I came to deliver a message." I walked forward, met his eyes. "Aengus. Listen to me. Listen well."

I didn't move until he acknowledged me. "I'm listening, I'm listening," he said.

I waited a moment longer before I spoke. "If

any harm comes to that man…any at all…" I trailed off, knowing Aengus would fill in the blanks.

"Are you talking about that witness that miraculously came to your rescue?" he said.

"You know exactly who I'm talking about. You'd better wish him a long life of good health. Because if anything happens to him, I'm taking it out on your ass," I said.

"I thought you made a promise. Aren't you a man of your word?" he said, throwing my promise in my face.

"I am, Aengus, but promises can be broken," I said, holding his gaze. "Not a single hair," I said.

A moment later, I turned and left.

THIRTY-TWO

EDEN

I had never been more exhausted or more exhil-
arated than I was after that morning in court.

During the week that Michael had been gone, I
had been an anxious mess, my gut churning, my
insides gnawing at me.

Now that things had been resolved, I felt wrung
out, the leftover adrenaline leaving me wrecked.

When Michael came in this time, I launched
myself at him again, not making any bones about
hugging him, letting him know how happy I was.

"That's all it takes to get that kind of greeting?"
he said.

I playfully smacked his arm and then looked up
at him.

"So you're a free man," I said.

"Yeah. Thanks to you," he said.

I frowned. "Me?"

"Yeah, turns out all that shit you nag me about was helpful. The maintenance man felt compelled to come forward because you treated him so well," Michael said.

"No, Michael. I didn't treat him so well. Any of them. You did."

He didn't agree, but he didn't refute what I said either. For a moment, we stood there embracing.

His eyes softened and he looked at me. "I'm glad you're okay," he said.

"Yeah, I'm glad you're okay too."

"Have you been to your house?" he asked.

"Yeah," I said on a deep sigh. "It's a total loss. They have to gut it. Thank God I have insurance," I said.

He shrugged. "Don't worry about it. I'm taking care of it," he said like it was nothing.

I tilted my head at him. "Michael, what does that mean?"

"I'll have it rebuilt," he said.

I looked at him, incredulous. "Michael, you're not building me a house."

"Of course not. I'm building us a house," he said.

"You're so... Wait, 'us'?" I asked, lifting a brow.

"Yeah. I was going to suggest we live in the condo, but you're stubborn as hell, so I know you'll want your house back," he said.

"So we're going to stay there together?"

"Obviously," he said.

"We? You want us to live together?"

"Yeah. Just like you do," he said.

"How do you know what I want?" I asked.

He looked at me, his expression impatient. "Eden, of course you want to live with me. You love me."

I looked at him, eyes wide. "Don't you think that's a little presumptuous?" I asked when I could finally speak.

"No. You love me, and I love you. So we'll live together."

At his words, my heart soared, making it almost impossible for me to give him crap.

Almost.

"If I didn't love you so much, I'd argue with you," I said.

He lifted a brow. "You should. I seem to recall enjoying how our arguments turn out."

EPILOGUE

HIM

FROM THE ASHES...

He looked at the newspaper headline, quickly read the story about the groundbreaking at the new M. Lounge and Hotel.

The old building had burned to the ground, but the Murphy brothers had wasted no time rebuilding. None of them had been interviewed for the article, but when he looked at the picture, he recognized the two oldest, the image blurry but not so much that he couldn't identify them.

He handed the newspaper to the guard, then leaned against the bars, the walls of his cage seeming to grow smaller each day.

He reminded himself this was temporary.

From the ashes.

Such an apt quote.

It seemed the Murphy brothers had gone through their fair share of challenges recently, but had had their triumphs too.

They were probably naive enough to think they had weathered the storm, come out on the other side.

He couldn't wait to show them how wrong they were.

———

Thank you for reading! Want more of the Murphys? CLICK HERE to order BIND, book three in the Irish Mob Chronicles!

A NOTE FROM KAYE

I hope you enjoyed *Reap!* And thank you for reading.

The Chronicles continue in *Bind*, book 3 of the series, **which you can order now.** I'm looking forward to continuing to explore the world of the Murphys, and you know I'm always hard at work on the next book, so **join my newsletter to be the first to know all about my upcoming releases!**

Can I ask a favor? Please leave a review for *Reap.* Whether you liked the book or not, your reviews give me and other readers really helpful feedback, and I appreciate each one.

Check out my website at **www.kayebluewriter.com**

to find out more about my books. And you can always find me on my Facebook page: **www.facebook.com/writerkayeblue** or on Instagram **@writerkayeblue.**

Till next time!

xo
Kaye

ROMANIAN MOB CHRONICLES

Keep

Fall

Avenge

Keep: The Wedding

War

Fight

Redeem

THORNEHILL SPRINGS

Two Weeks in Geneva: Complete Series

Where You Least Expect

Who You Least Expect

When You Least Expect

MEN WHO THRILL

The Enforcer

The Assassin

The Soldier

The Con

PLAYTHINGS

Devil's Plaything

Demon's Plaything

Elah's Plaything

Made in the USA
Middletown, DE
18 May 2023

30863408R00203